D.A. ALSTON

Royal Elite Squad: Fiery Daze

Contents

Acknowledgement

I thought really hard about who I was going to dedicate this book to. *Royal Elite Squad: Fiery Daze* literally took me through the fire to create it. There were often times where I wanted to give up. Times I figured I was one and done. However, I was blessed with so many reminders that I needed to keep going.

Shoutout to my students from my *Just Write* workshops and the Boys & Girls Club. You all experienced my book firsthand. You encouraged me, became my biggest cheerleaders and even played a major role in character development like picking the supervillan's name (thank you McKenzie).

Many of my friends patiently listened to drafts of my book and ideas into the wee hours of the night and never complained. This book is bits and pieces of all of us. My family, friends, students and all the people I've encountered, past and present. This book would not have happened without the support, ideas and inspiration from you all.

Thank you from the bottom of my heart,
  —D.A. Alston

Chapter 1

Janais

I was suffocating. I was surrounded by hundreds of people, and somehow, I still felt terribly alone. My wrist ached from all the hands I had shaken this evening and all the *hellos* and *nice-to-meet-yous* made my full lips numb.

"Well, aren't you rather pretty for a dark-skinned girl?" asked a silver-haired lady resembling the Queen of England as she reached out to touch my perfectly sculpted fro. "It's just so... *big!*"

I quickly jerked away from her withered fingers. "No one touches the crown!" I snapped, folding my arms.

Just then, my mother began pinching the back of my arm with such force, I felt blood loss. "We're so sorry, Mrs. Caldwell. My daughter had a long day and is probably lacking sleep, hence her attitude. We thank you for coming to support my husband and I." Mrs. Caldwell simply stuck her nose up prudishly and turned to leave, whipping her elegant gown around behind her. I looked up slowly to see my mother's eyes glaring down on me as if I was staring into the barrel of a gun. "We'll talk about this later," she whispered through the crack of her flawlessly applied Mac lipstick as she began to walk away. The distance between my mother and myself continued to grow as she found a more important cause: talking money out of guilty millionaires who thought throwing their funds at the less fortunate would somehow gain them access to a heaven of some sorts.

I found an empty table where I could sit and I began stuffing my mouth with cocktail shrimp. The boredom was extremely real. It was only Wednesday, but it was the third event I'd been to this week. It was honestly getting to the point where it was too much. I watched my parents parade around the room and rub elbows with Atlanta's finest. Between my mother and father, I wasn't sure who the bigger actor was. They both seemed to play a role to get what they wanted. My dad was searching for political advancement while my mother thought she could save the world with donations and nonprofits.

BUZZ BUZZ

I glanced at the phone hoping for relief from the mundane shindig. To my excitement, it was a video call from my best friend Libby Gray. A loud noise exploded from my phone after I tapped the answer key. It was a song that I couldn't quite make out because the volume on her end was so loud. Embarrassment washed all over my face as everyone in the conference room began to search frantically for the source of the disruption. Before anyone could voice their disappointment, I got up and ran through the wooden double doors, finding refuge in a deserted back hall.

"Hello! Hello! Nay! Where are you?" she yelled, overpowering her still roaring music. The song changed but it was equally as loud. I sat on the floor and placed my headphones in my ears.

"Yes, Libs, I'm here. Sorry, I am still at this event for my parents," I sighed.

"You're *still* there?" Libby Gray groaned, taking a break from painting. "Didn't it start like six hours ago?"

I looked at the clock. *Midnight.* All I could do was sigh. "Yeah, more or less…" I shrugged, attempting to get comfortable.

"More, Nay! More!" Libs laughed before putting her serious face on. "But aren't you excited we'll be back at our own school next week? There is nothing to do at this new school but pay attention. Can you believe I have a B in Science right now? I am just excited to be on spring break! Relaxing and doing nothing is more my speed."

It had been six months since *the incident* forced our school, Ridgewood Junior High, to close down. The time had flown by, but it would be back to our normal lives soon. Well, as normal as life could be for super-powered teens.

"Nayyyyy," Libby Gray yelled, bringing my attention back to the conversation.

"My bad, I'm here!" I apologized.

"Well, yeah I know you're there. I can see you," Libby Gray laughed. "Where did your mind go? You're always in the clouds these days." I simply stared at her blankly. "Come on, you can talk to me. You've been distant from everyone lately. Adeema and Kenzie agree. We're just worried about you," Libs said concerned.

"Well, no one asked you to worry about me," I snapped back. "I'm fine like I said."

"Sheesh, Nay. I was just trying to help," Libby Gray said. "But forget it. I'll talk to you later when you don't have a major attitude!"

Before I could apologize, she hung up and I was left looking at the home screen. It was a picture of Kenzie, Adeema, Libs, and I. *What was wrong with me?* I was so distraught lately. Every other minute, it felt like 150,000 watts were surging through my veins. I was a ticking time bomb waiting to explode.

Adeema

"She's guarded all around. Only five seconds left on the clock. Hatem breaks left, breaks right, goes up and it's... *GOOD!* The crowd goes wild. The three-point queen does it again!" I screamed, jumping around my backyard as if I was in an arena filled with thousands of people. Sweat rolled down my forehead, escaping my tightly-wrapped hijab. The April showers left the so air thick and humid, that playing ball was mostly unbearable, but it was my sanctuary.

"Adeema, you have a visitor," my mother said, peeking from behind the screen door.

I looked up and saw a long slender girl skipping up. *"Hola chica!"* Kenzie smiled.

I smiled before glancing down at my sweaty clothes. "I would hug you, but—"

"No worries, I wasn't even going to ask." Kenzie laughed, grabbing the basketball rolling aimlessly on the ground and throwing it in the air. "I can always count on you to be playing with this thing."

"I have to stay in shape all the time. We never know when the next attack will happen," I said, sitting on the ground. "But what's up? You didn't even call. A lot has to be on your mind if you just came over."

"You know me well," Kenzie said, trying to make a shot but failing terribly. She dug her freshly manicured hands in her oversized UCLA hoodie and laid back on the grass. "Have you talked to Janais lately?

I laid back and looked at the clouds in the sky, trying to recall the last time I spoke to her. "Man, I don't know, it's been awhile honestly. I invited her to go to Little 5 Points for National Comic Book Day, but she flaked on me," I said, wrapping my fingers together up under my head.

"*Que pasando?* She has been avoiding me a lot too. Even Libs said something seems to be up," Kenzie sighed.

"That's not like Nay. Maybe we'll find out more after the sleepover this weekend," I said, rolling over to my side. "Plus, we'll be back to school next week! No more spring break."

"Chill! Don't talk about going back to school just yet. I don't want to hear about school right now. My brain can't take anymore algorithms, new cheers or projects. I am ready to do nothing, but be a regular teen," Kenzie laughed, throwing her hands in the air.

"You mean a regular teen *with superpowers*, right? " I snickered, looking over as Kenzie levitated a water bottle, the basketball and her purse.

"Oh, yeah!" she laughed as everything fell to the ground.

"What else has been going on with you? How's your brother doing lately?" I asked, scrolling through my phone.

She sighed. "As okay as someone can be who has cancer in the majority of his body. One day, he's great—the next, not so much."

I wanted her to elaborate, but I sensed she wanted me to let it be, so I did. I heard a loud commotion coming from inside the house that redirected my attention. "What's going on?" I inquired, leaning up.

"Let's go check it out, " Kenzie insisted. We got up from the hot ground and made our way inside. I could hear my sisters and my mother yelling.

"Another one?" Amani screamed.

"This is awful," my mother said, sitting on the couch.

The ruckus echoed throughout the halls. They were yelling at the news segment so loudly, I could barely tell what it was about.

"What's going on?" I asked as I sat on the La-Z-Boy.

"It's the High Museum of Art! It burned down! A lot of people are hurt, some even died," Amara said, sitting on the arm of my chair with her eyes glued to the TV.

"Oh, *dios mio!* Another fire? What's up with Georgia and these outbreaks?" Kenzie asked, sitting on the floor in front of the TV.

Our last mission had involved fire. People had been so amazed at how the fire on the Highway 85 Bridge didn't harm anyone—little did they know it was because four fly girls had been on the case.

"This is the second fire at an Atlanta museum. Police officials are starting to think an arsonist is involved instead of the previous assumption that it was a gas leak," the news anchor explained. We stared at the TV screen as the video played over and over. The fire moved around the building erratically. It was chaotic yet serene. Who knew such pain and destruction could have that much beauty in it?

Libby Gray

Amy Winehouse's "Valerie" echoed in the walls of my room as I floated across my chevron rug spinning and singing terribly.

"Storm! Turn that ruckus down!" I heard my father yell from down the hall. I ignored his request and continued to parade around my room without a care in the world. Honestly, I had a few, but I wouldn't worry about them until after the song went off. Each hair on my head danced around to its own rhythm yet all in sync. It was organized chaos like a wildfire. My hands clapped together on the two and four. My feet moved so quickly I barely touched the ground—I was flying. This was my happy, this was my safe. Nothing could change how I felt. Or so I thought.

Reality crashed through my room like a wrecking ball reminding me that I could not fly. The wrecking ball was none other than my father, Colonel Dawson. "What did I tell you about this ruckus, Storm?" he yelled, turning off my stereo.

"I'm sorry, Poppa. I—"

"Just shut up! What are you even doing in this room?" he asked. Before I could even say anything, he pushed my stereo system onto the floor as he tried to catch his balance.

"Poppa! Are you okay?"

"I'm fine! I'm fine!" He looked around in his head, searching for the next part of his deranged rant. "What was I saying?" His eyes lit up when he found the runaway train of his thoughts. "Clean up this mess and quit dancing around like a crazed hippie! Do something with your life already!" he yelled, slamming the door behind him and leaving me standing there.

It didn't feel like I was flying anymore. I was sinking. No longer did I feel safe, let alone happy. I looked up to the sky, fighting the urge to cry. I tried to justify that it was normal. It wasn't his fault. This was just how he got after he came back from fighting overseas. It would get better. I knew it would.

I laid down on my bed and picked up my phone right as I was receiving a call from Adeema. I took a deep breath and shook off what was going on before answering the phone. "Hey, there!" I said, giving my best *everything-is-okay-and-I-was-definitely-not-just-crying* voice.

"Hey, Libs! Are you busy?" Adeema asked.

"Too busy for you? Never," I said, getting comfortable on my bed.

"That's great. Have you been watching the news these past few days?"

"Why on Earth would I watch the news on purpose? It's uneventful at best."

"The news is very informative! How can you not—you know what? Never mind. Kenzie and I think something is going on. Want to meet at Oak Park at four to discuss it?"

"This isn't another one of your imaginary new missions, is it? 'Cause I would rather not spend my spring break on a wild goose chase." This wasn't the first time Adeema had made something up in her mind. She was becoming slightly obsessed with new missions.

"It was only twice, Libs! Not cool!" she laughed. "But for real, meet us at four—even Janais agreed to come."

"Fine, fine! I'll be there. I guess the Squad is really back together, huh?"

"Yes, indeed. Now start getting dressed! You know it takes you three hours to get ready and it's already 2," Adeema said.

I was going to combat her statement, but realized she was telling the truth. "Alright, I'll see ya later," I said before hanging up. I hopped out of bed and started looking for something to wear. My army fatigue jumpsuit was the first thing to catch my eye, playing peek-a-boo in between my other clothes.

I smiled and decided on something a little less obvious. I quickly grabbed my favorite pair of distressed jeans that always made my legs look great and a cute neon crop top. Now the only things left were to find shoes and pick out accessories. "Dang it! What am I going to do with my hair?" I asked aloud, catching a glimpse of myself in my mirror. *Yep, I am definitely going to be late.*

Kenzie

The park felt damp from the sporadic rain storms Georgia was infamous for. Thankfully, the worst of it had ended a little over an hour ago. My head bobbed to the melody of the high school band playing in the distance. My fingers fiddled around mid-air as if I was playing my trumpet along with them and my legs swung off the park table I was sitting on. The percussion section joined in as all the individual parts came together to form the epitome of 'One Band, One Sound.' They played effortlessly as Bruno Mars' "That's What I Like" rang throughout the park. I got so caught up with the music, I almost forgot why I had originally shown up. It wasn't until I looked up and saw the vague silhouettes of Libby Gray, Adeema and Janais approaching that I remembered.

"I think I deserve a sticker or a cookie or something!" Libby Gray said, taking a seat on the bench. "I made it here right when everyone else did!"

"Libs has a point—she is normally the last one here," Adeema laughed. "She deserves some kind of prize,"

Janais threw a piece of gum at Libby Gray and we all exploded with laughter. "I'm slightly offended... what are you trying to say? Does my breath stink? " Libby Gray laughed as she opened the gum and popped it in her mouth unapologetically.

"It's all I had! You asked for a treat—it was that or a Chick-fil-A mint." Janais giggled, sitting at the table. Everyone got comfortable. This place felt like home even though it had been months since we all met at the table. Alas, it was time to get to work.

"So, what was so urgent we had to meet here today?" Libby Gray asked, scrolling through Instagram.

Adeema motioned me to go on. "Well, we were watching the news this morning and something weird is going on. There was another fire at a museum... this time, there were a lot of people injured and even some casualties," I explained, showing Janais and Libby Gray a video of the fire.

"We may have abilities, but that doesn't mean we can stop random anomalies," Janais said, cutting her eyes at Adeema and I.

I ignored her sass. "Except it wasn't random. Even the police don't think it's a gas leak anymore. Someone must be doing this! And who better to stop them than us?" I asked proudly. I stood up to await their response, but the girls grew quiet. Seconds turned into minutes, yet no one spoke. I decided to break the silence. "So, what do y'all think? The suspense is killing me."

Libby Gray reluctantly pulled her eyes away from her phone. "I don't know... seems like a stretch to me. Y'all are probably making something out of nothing." I couldn't believe my ears. I looked over to Janais who had her head down on the table with her headphones in.

"Janais, um... what about you? People are getting hurt. We have to do something, right?" I pleaded with her.

"Eh, it's whatever you all decide," Janais said with a shrug, barely making eye contact. I looked at Adeema who was as dumbfounded as I was. The Royal Elite Squad was disconnected. We weren't a unit anymore. Time had done a number on us.

"Janais, what's been up with you lately? This passive aggressive crap isn't cutting it anymore. You're just plain on being rude!" Adeema said, slamming her hand on the park table with so much force, it left an imprint on the table. Janais slowly removed her headphones one-by-one and looked at Adeema who was staring her down.

"Oh Lord, don't start that," Libby Gray said, rolling her emerald eyes. "You know she doesn't want to talk to us about what is going on her head. Even though we're *supposed* to be best friends."

"Excuse me then! Since I am such a problem, I think I should eliminate myself from the equation," Janais said, standing up from the table and turning to leave. "If I wanted to feel like an outcast, I would have stayed home!"

"Janais, wait—!" Adeema yelled, but she was gone like a lightning bolt. *Here one second, gone the next.* She turned back to us. "Go after her, Libby Gray!"

"Why should I? She doesn't want to be bothered and I'm honestly tired of begging. I'm over it." Libby Gray said before poofing away, leaving nothing but the red residue from her hair in the air.

I bit my lip and fought back tears. People were dying and we were fighting with each other over the pettiest things.

"You gonna be okay?" Adeema asked, placing her hand on my shoulder. I nodded. "I need to go release some frustration—don't worry Kenzie... they'll come back around," she said with a hug.

I was so frustrated I couldn't even muster up a good bye as she began to walk away. I sat back down on the bench, placed my head down and listened to the band play again with a heavy sigh. Saving the world was going to be a lot harder this time around.

Chapter 2

Janais

I laid on my bed, staring at the overnight bag I had packed earlier in the week. It was 9:00 o'clock Friday morning and I still hadn't made up my mind if I would be attending our end of spring break sleepover. I hadn't even talked to them since I stormed out yesterday. Adeema had called six times last night and texted at least twenty times trying to check in on me. Kenzie tried to video chat me as well, but Libby Gray hadn't reached out at all. I couldn't blame her though. I began maneuvering miniate surges of energy between my fingers, one of the few things that calmed me as of late. I hummed a melody that my mother would sing when I used to lay in her lap many moons ago. She would rub her fingers through my hair and everything at that moment would seem right.

KNOCK KNOCK

"It's locked!" I yelled without even bothering to open my eyes. I hoped whoever it was would get the picture and come back another time. Unfortunately, I heard the door swing open instead.

"Now child, you know I have a key to every door in this

house, right? It is *my* house, after all," my mother announced, marching through the door. I didn't even bother trying to come up with a rebuttal—she would win every time and I knew it. "Why are all the lights off in here and why aren't you dressed yet? You know we have a brunch to go to in an hour."

"Do I have to go?" I whined, hoping for once I wouldn't be have to be designated as the token black girl who studied, got good grades and talked 'white' for nothing more than a spectacle. It was honestly starting to feel like the only reason I was there—I could show the potential donors that inner city youth could be successful too if only they applied themselves. *Their words, not mine.* I looked at my mother who was fluffing her golden-brown curls in the mirror. You couldn't deny my mother's beauty. Even Stevie Wonder could attest.

"Come on, sweetheart! It'll be fun... I promise. We'll even get your favorite ice cream afterwards if it'll appease your spirits, my dear," she said, turning around to gaze at me with a warmth I hadn't felt in a while.

"Marable Slab? Really?" I asked, finally sitting up. She nodded and smiled before heading into my walk-in closet, beginning to pick through my clothes. I guess it was mother's choice for brunch.

"I know we've been busy raising money for all the nonprofits and you're still such a little girl, you may not understand why I work as hard as I do. But I promise this is all for you," she said, placing an outfit on the bed. "Now, get ready sweetheart. We have to leave soon." She left the room as gracefully as she entered. I stood up and saw the outfit she picked out.

I felt something within me rising. My blood had been ignited by the electricity intertwined in my DNA and drowning in my emotions. I was being suffocated by silence. I was no better than a puppet. I had no control over my life, only being pulled and pushed in whatever way everyone else decided. I grabbed the 'perfect' outfit my mother picked out. I sent a few thousand bolts of electricity through the dress.

"I'm done being their cookie cutter girl," I said, throwing the ashes into my metal trash can.

Adeema

"We still have no major leads on the cause of the fire at the High Museum of Art, but we're told officials are doing everything possible to find the cause. The victims' families from this terrible incident have started demanding answers. Protestors have lined up at the steps of City Hall and they are not pleased with the police for not having the answers they seek." It was the third time I had watched the news segment video. I was hoping I would find something to help further my unction that we needed to do something, but alas, all I heard was hearsay. I knew the fires had to be connected somehow, but I couldn't figure out what it was. Normally this was where Libby Gray and Janais would chime in using social media and their brain power to find the root of the problem. This time it was only me.

I began brainstorming my thoughts on paper. If the group wouldn't figure it out, I would do it myself. "Okay, what do I know?" I said aloud in my best Kenzie voice. "There have been fires at the High Museum of Art, Atlanta History Museum, the bridge on 85 and one at Piedmont Park. That's four fires in a three-month span. " A text from my mother flashed across my phone, breaking my concentration. *Adeema, the men are here to fix your bedroom lights. Get ready!* I guess saving the world would have to wait. I quickly grabbed a scarf from my closet and headed to the bathroom. I looked at myself in the mirror and began wrapping my hijab around my head. I tucked the little flyaway hairs back under the multicolored scarf that had escaped. I took a deep breath and smiled. "Perfect," I said to myself before heading downstairs.

My father was talking to the handymen as my mother sat on the couch, reading a book. My mother's eyes met mine and she smiled with approval. My house was filled with so many people, from the workers to my family, and even my brother was back from college. I needed space to breathe. I headed outside. Maybe the outdoors would help me focus on all that was going on with the fires.

I picked up my basketball and began dribbling it around the driveway. *I might as well work on my jumper.*

Before I could even go up for a shot, I heard a loud obnoxious voice barking from behind. "Oh, look guys... the Taliban is trying to play *my* game!" I rolled my eyes before turning around, knowing it was Helga Shayṭān. For someone who had fought countless bad guys over the past few months with ease, I suddenly felt stricken with nervousness and fear. Helga had been making my entire middle school experience a living hell. I was relieved when I found out we would be going to different schools after the explosion and I prayed I would never see her again. But alas, here she was standing in front of me with her minions. "You not going to say anything?"

"Hi Helga," I mumbled, staring at the ground.

"WELL, WHAT DO YOU KNOW? IT SPEAKS ENGLISH TOO!" she laughed. I looked around outside hoping for some relief as Helga and her friends walked towards me. I looked back and the door was at least ten feet away. I could make a dash for it, but it could possibly reveal my abilities.

"Why do you look so scared?" the short blonde asked.

"She probably thinks we're going to ship her back to Iraq," Helga said, cracking her knuckles in her hands. "She's probably an illegal anyway… maybe we should call ICE." I began to grow angry at their insults and started to wrestle with if I should beat them within an inch of their lives like the stereotypical violent Muslim they already perceived me to be. Or I could remain still and try to act like it didn't bother me and risk getting beat up. I battled in my mind what I was going to do next.

Before I could think of a good solution to the brewing problem, my brother Aameen walked outside. "Adeema, are you okay?" he yelled from the door entrance as the girls halted in their steps.

"Uh yeah," I yelled back, hoping he would detect the uneasiness in my voice.

"It's about time to eat—come on in," my brother said.

"This isn't over," Helga said under her breath before turning to walk away.

I stood there frozen as tears began rolling down my apple cheeks. *How could people be so cruel?* And all because I looked different. I dropped the ball I was holding and covered my face to mask my frustration. Soon thereafter, I felt a warm embrace.

"Not out here you don't," he said, leading me inside. "Never let them see you cry, 'Deema." I tried with all my force to stop crying ,but I just couldn't. Here I was with all these abilities and I still couldn't help being stricken with fear by a girl who could only dribble a ball.

Libby Gray

I browsed through my favorite store, Forever21, singing along with Dua Lipa as I indulged in some retail therapy. I picked through the clearance section since my allowance had been kind of scarce lately. I noticed some girls off in the corner looking in my direction, but simply rolled my eyes and kept shopping. I stumbled upon a pair of beautifully distressed jean shorts with fringe at the bottom. My eyes grew so big, they could have popped out my head as I held them in the air to get a better view. I took out my phone to snap a photo for my Instagram with the caption *Have you ever seen anything anymore Libby Gray?*

"Those can't be for her, can they?" I overheard one of the girls say with a laugh. She's way too big to be wearing things like that."

I was used to these kinds of comments, but for some reason, I felt incredibly shocked at the girls' nerve. "Excuse me, I couldn't hear you," I said with my arms folded, waiting for one of them to say something out of pocket so I could go off. "Speak up this time when you talk your trash."

The group of girls laughed. "Chill, it wasn't that serious. You should learn to take a joke like you take a Big Mac."

"Was that a fat joke? Y'all must do better than that. Fat isn't synonymous for ugly, 'cause clearly, I'm a work of art. And skinny doesn't mean beautiful; for example, *you four*. I've seen better faces on The Walking Dead." They stared at me dumbfounded. "Now hurry on, this fat girl has some clothes to try on." I turned dramatically and walked towards the dressing room. I took a deep breath and tried to compose myself. I hated bullies. I forced a smile on my face and shook off my discomfort once again.

I looked down to see an unexpected call coming in: Janais. I hadn't talked to her since the blow up. I was trying to give her the space I thought she wanted.

I was just about to answer when I heard a soft voice behind me. "Hey Libs," Janais said, phone in one hand as she fidgeted with her jacket zipper in the other.

"What are you doing here?"

"I know I'm the last person you'd expect to see..."

"What's been going on with you?"

"Going on with me?"

She was playing dumb. "What you're not going to do is come at me with nonsense when I was just trying to help fix whatever was—"

"I DIDN'T ASK YOU TO FIX ME!" Janais yelled out. Silence grew between us. I saw the pain in her eyes. I looked around to see everyone in the store staring at us.

"Excuse me, is everything okay?" an older woman with a Forever 21 badge asked, walking up to us. Before I could reply, Janais bolted for the door, knocking down countless clothes in her path. I looked around and saw the whole store staring, holding onto every word as if it were a life vest and they were drowning.

"I'm sorry!" I exclaimed abruptly, giving the lady the clothes I was about to try on. I rushed out the store hoping to find Janais. I scanned over the hundreds of people who were in sight. None matched Janais' description. There had to be a better way to find her. "If I were Janais, where would I be?" I said aloud, looking at the mall map display. My anxiety was full on at this point. *What if I can't find her? What if our friendship is beyond repair?* I thought to myself.

Then it hit me! She always goes to the Cinnabon next to the

art gallery when she's stressed. Eating sweets and looking at high end art always seemed to calm her down—it was actually one of the things which made me love her, because I did the same thing. I jetted to the escalator as soon as the idea formed in my head. The Cinnabon was on the first floor. I ran down the right wing of the wall. I could see her off in the distance, staring into the gallery display, stuffing her mouth. I stopped running when I was only a few feet away. I begin walking towards her as I adjusted my clothes.

I stood next to her as she stared at an Edvard Munch piece. At the moment, his art was making more sense than whatever was going on with us. I was waiting for the right moment to say something. Time slowed down so much, I thought Mrs. Jones was around. I gazed at her as she finished her churro. *Now or never*, I thought to myself. "Look Nay, I'm—"

My apology was halted by a combustion inside the gallery. A young lady ran out the gallery, wailing at the top of her lungs "FIRE! FIREEEEE!"

Janais and I instantly went into hero mode, running inside the gallery to see if we could help. The heat was unbearable. Smoke from the flames began to spread and make the air almost unbreathable.

"Help! Help!" a woman cried between coughs as she hid under a table.

"I got her!" Janais said, using her speed to grab her quickly and place her outside. Thankfully, the smog was getting so thick so no one could see her use her lightning speed. Janais continued to help get the remaining people out. I decided to try to find the source of the fire and any remaining people before the whole gallery was a pile of ash. I walked behind the counter to see if someone was hiding behind there. There was cloudy image of a boy squatting down.

"I'm here to help," I said, reaching out my hand.

The boy quickly stood up, towering over me. "I didn't ask for a hero," he said, creating some sort of fire-powered ball of energy in his hands.

"Libs? Where are you?" I heard Janais yell out. Before I could answer, the boy's ball of energy knocked me into the wall. I let out a groan and tried to jump out of the gallery, but I was too weak. I saw Janais running towards me. "OMG Libs, are you—" She didn't even have a chance to see what was coming as the blurry image threw another fire ball in her direction, knocking her against the wall as well.

I couldn't fight anymore. Between the fumes and the unbearable pain I was in, I could barely keep my eyes open. All I could do was black out.

Kenzie

I paced the floor, trying to keep myself busy from thinking the worst. The stench of stale tears, latex gloves, tapioca pudding and bleach engulfed the halls. This is what I imagined most hospitals smelled like. We were playing the waiting game, and to be frank, I was losing. *What was taking so long? Why couldn't we go in yet? What really happened?* The only solace I had was sitting in the waiting room with me praying.

"*Siéntate, McKenzie!*" my mother insisted, tapping the chair beside her.

"How can I sit at a time like this?" I whined, walking in circles. My mother snapped her fingers and pointed to the chair again with a look I didn't have the energy to test. I plopped in the seat between her and Adeema who had just finished praying. "I just wish I had been there. Maybe we wouldn't be sitting in a hospital, waiting to see if our friends are okay."

"Oh sweetheart," my mother said, pulling me closer. "It was just a terrible accident. You couldn't have saved them—you're not a super hero." She combed my hair with her fingers, and I sighed as my mother's embrace calmed me for a brief second.

"I'm looking for a McKenzie Vega and Adeema Hatem," a nurse with SpongeBob scrubs announced to the waiting room.

We popped up instantly. "That's us!" we exclaimed in unison.

"This way please," the nurse said, guiding us through the automatic door as our mothers nudged us to go on. We both quickly kissed their cheeks before rushing to meet the nurse. We walked past countless injured individuals. Grady Hospital was known for treating trauma victims and they were living up to that. She stopped in front of a door before pushing it open. "You have two very blessed young ladies who have been asking to see you in Room 118. Go ahead!" I followed Adeema through the room.

"FINALLY!!! You're here!" Libby Gray yelled out, taking a break from her cup of red Jell-O. Adeema ran to hug Libby Gray as I grabbed Janais who happened to be looking out the window when we came in.

"We've been freaking out! What happened? We've been out in the waiting room for hours!" I said pulling back a bit, so I wouldn't suffocate Janais.

"Breathe Kenz!" Adeema laughed.

"I'm sorry!" I said, plopping down Libby Gray's bed. Kenzie grabbed my hand and I looked down to see it bruised. I felt tears begin to form in my eyes.

"No, we're not doing that!" Libby Gray said with a hug. "We're alive—this is a good moment."

"So, what happened exactly?" Adeema asked, taking a seat next to Janais. "We heard about the fire at the museum. It sounds like it was a crazy accident."

Janais took a deep breath and looked at the door to make sure the coast was clear. "It wasn't an accident," she whispered.

"What do you mean?" I asked, amazed that my friends had just gone through so much.

"I didn't... well, *we* didn't see it before. But you both may actually be on to something," Libby Gray said. I was still a little confused.

"It was no accident—someone caused the fire," Janais said.

I couldn't believe what I was hearing. Adeema and I were right. She nudged Libby Gray to go on. "We have to find him. " Libby Gray said

"*Him?*" Adeema and I said in unison.

Chapter 3

"Are you sure you are ready to go back to school?" my mom asked, sitting on my bed while I packed my bookbag. "The doctors gave you a few days off to get back adjusted—why not take it?"

I had been stuck at home with my parents for two days straight, and to my surprise, I was starting to miss the silence of being alone. "No ma'am, I miss my friends and my school." My mother simply sighed. "Plus, I'll go crazy if I'm in this house another day," I mumbled under my breath.

"What did you say?" she snapped.

"Oh nothing," I said, grabbing my bag. "I'll see you later!" I said, running to meet Libby Gray and her brother who were waiting outside to take me to school. I threw my bag in the back of his new Jeep Cherokee, a present from Mr. & Mrs. Dawson for getting into six of the eight colleges he'd applied to. No more being cramped in the back of his old car that was held together by a wish and a prayer. Libby Gray looked back at me from the passenger's seat and gave the biggest smile imaginable, showing off her Grand Canyon dimples. We hadn't really discussed the mall incident yet, but I knew our petty argument could wait.

"Seat belts!" CJ yelled, tapping the steering wheel. I quickly obliged and laid back in my seat. Libby Gray started singing obnoxiously along to the radio as I gazed out the window. I was mentally exhausted—after all, being almost burned alive was a lot for anyone to handle. We had to figure out who this mystery person was before more people got hurt.

"What class do you have first, Nay?" Libby Gray asked, interrupting the concert she was putting on.

I grabbed my phone and opened my school email that had our new schedules in it. "Looks like Science, Room 243: Mrs. Jones" I was so glad she was coming back! She made Ridgewood so much better.

"I got Mrs. Jones too!" Libby Gray said, looking back at me. "Ayyyyy, it's going to be lit!"

"Don't do that," I said, cutting my eyes at her. "It's too early in the morning for appropriation."

"My bad! You know I get caught up sometimes." I loved Libby Gray, but sometimes she tried a little too hard.

"We're here!" CJ said, hitting the brakes so hard it jerked me forward. "Y'all weirdos get out." Thankfully, I had on my seatbelt or I may have been resting on the hood of the car. I grabbed my bag and quickly got out the car, heading to the sidewalk as Libby Gray hopped out after me. We linked arms and headed towards the building.

"Is your brother always a jerk?" I asked, looking up at the new and improved Ridgewood Middle School.

"Yup! I think he has a chemical imbalance in his head," Libby Gray said, rolling her eyes. "I want my parents to get him tested, but they refuse," We walked through the halls of our once fallen school. Everyone seemed to miss someone as I noticed a number of people run up to hug one another. It was well into the second semester, but it almost felt like the beginning of the school year.

"Future ninth graders, remember to visit the counselor's office today to pick your classes for next year, " the announcements screeched through the intercom.

"Quit running!" Coach Smith yelled down the hall at the boys playing some form of tag.

"Janais!" I heard someone scream out from behind.

"Libs!" another familiar voice yelled out. We both turned around to find Adeema and Kenzie running up to us and giving us a tight squeeze.

"Not so rough, Adeema!" I laughed. "I still have some bandages under here."

"Oops! I forget my own strength sometimes." We all linked arms and headed down the hall.

"I am glad we're all back together," Kenzie said, placing her head on my shoulder.

"Please tell me you all have Mrs. Jones first period, too," Libby Gray said.

"You know it! We're back with our favorite teacher!" Adeema said, linking her arm in Libby Gray's.

"Do you think we should tell her about... *you know what?*" Kenzie asked.

We all cut our eyes at her. "Shhhhh!" Libby Gray, Adeema and I shushed in unison.

"No hero talk in public," Adeema whispered.

"*Lo siento*," Kenzie said. "I just want to get to the bottom of this flame-throwing jerk. Now, more than ever."

We made our way through the cluttered halls and found our way to class. Mrs. Jones was busy writing on the board dressed in a fluffy polka-dot skirt, sparkly blue chuck Taylors, a blue Marvel superhero shirt and a black blazer. She's the only one who could pull of something so eclectic.

"Mrs. Jones!" Libby Gray screamed, following me into the classroom.

"Good Morning, Ms. Dawson. I'm happy to see you're so energized for science this morning," Mrs. Jones said, turning from the dry erase board as her eyes peeked over her red-horned glasses and a smirk crept across her face.

"See, I didn't say all that... I'm just excited to see you, that's all. I still very much hate science" Libby Gray said with a laugh before finding her usual seat towards the back of the class.

Mrs. Jones shook her head and looked at me. She was doing that thing where I felt like she was reading my mind. I wouldn't be as nervous if she didn't have emphatic abilities.

"Hi, Mrs. Jones! Cool shirt," I said, trying to break her concentration.

"Thank you," Mrs. Jones said, stepping a little closer to me. "And how are you, dear... *really?*"

"I'm fine," I said quickly before taking a seat. "Promise." I didn't have the time to have an existential break down before first period.

She just looked at me and smiled sweetly before closing the door. "Okay class, that's the bell. It's time to begin!"

Libby Gray

The novelty of being back at school with all my friends dwindled with each second that passed on the clock. Mrs. Jones was at the front of the class rambling on about deoxyribonucleic acid in relation to genetics and I noticed this weird kid picking a scab on his arm. Janais was doing that thing where she tried to act like she wasn't stressed and Adeema was bouncing around imaginary basketballs. Kenzie was one of the few who was actually engaged. I just continued to wait for an interesting part of the lecture. To pass time, I doodled in my notebook, fleshing out a few new suit ideas I'd had in my head. It was about time for a new look for us, especially since we had a new villain on our hands. He had to be stopped before all of Georgia ended up in ashes.

"Ms. Dawson, would you like to add anything?" Mrs. Jones asked, interrupting my thoughts.

I looked up to see everyone staring at me. "Uhm, no ma'am, Mrs. Jones," I said, forcing a smile. "You're doing such an excellent job. I'll just let you continue" Mrs. Jones folded her arms and shook her head. Since Mrs. Jones was clearly in one of those calling-random-people-out moods, I decided to try and focus.

Just then, Josh raised his hand. "Mrs. Jones, is DNA and all that connected with our personalities too?"

"Excellent question! A lot of who we are is made up through-out genetics, but there is a century-old debate over nature versus nurture. Does anyone know what that means?" Janais and Kenzie's hands popped up simultaneously. "Yes Kenzie?"

"Isn't it about whether human behavior is determined by the environment or the genetics passed down from their parents?" Kenzie answered with that 'I-already-know-I'm-right' smile.

"That's correct. A lot of who you are is made up through genetics passed from you biological parents, but some can also be learned traits from your environment." The class grew quiet thinking on what she'd just said and I did the same. *I wonder where I get my crazy rebellious side from? Where did my creativity and need to experiment with life drive come from?* Finally, Mrs. Jones went on. "Your homework assignment—" The classroom let out a collective sigh. "It's not a hard one, I promise. I just want you to go home this evening and talk to your family about genetics and things that may have possibly passed down to you... and maybe even a few things that didn't. Everyone understand?" The class nodded. "Okay, I'll let you have the remaining ten minutes to discuss genetics with your classmates and whatever else might be trending right now."

The class quickly broke up into groups and mostly discussed everything but genetics. I grabbed my belongings and headed up to the front of the class where Janais and Kenzie were sitting as Adeema followed suit.

"I know I got my dark brown hair from my abeula," Kenzie said as I sat my things on a table before plopping myself on it as well. "My parents both have sandy brown hair unlike mine. What about you, Nay? What do you think you got from your parents?"

"My parents are fairly light-skinned, so I don't think my rich complexion came from them—probably someone further back."

"You certainly don't have your dad's grey eyes," Adeema chimed. "And aren't your mom's hazel? You don't have those either."

"Must have skipped a generation," she said, forcing a laugh.

"Well, red hair runs in my family," I jumped in. "The curls come from my momma's side though."

"All the women in my family have full lips and dark features," Adeema said. "And now that I think about it, the women in my family are all pretty hairy too—you should see my sisters' arms before wax day," she said with a laugh.

We chatted more about our similarities and differences until the bell rang. "Okay ladies and gents, remember your assignment," Mrs. Jones said, opening the door. "See you tomorrow!" Our classmates charged towards the door while the girls and I lingered around a little bit longer.

"So, what do you all have next?" Kenzie asked looking at her schedule on her phone

"Chorus," Janais said, putting her belongings in her bag.

"What? Are you for real?" I said, failing to contain my excitement. I looked around to see my friends equally as excited. We all knew Janais was the best singer at Ridgewood, but she was also terribly shy and often refused to sing in front of other people.

"That's major, chicka!" Kenzie said, hugging her tightly. "I'm so proud of you!"

"It's no big deal," Janais laughed. "It was either that or robotics, and I've already been the Young Robotics champ three years in a row, so I decided to do something different."

"Nonetheless, we're happy," Adeema interjected. "But I have gym. I have to get some conditioning in for next season."

"I have fine arts. I need to flesh out this abstract piece that is forming in my head." I said, thinking on all the different colors I was planning to use.

"And I have Honors English—looks like we're all going different ways," Kenzie sighed.

"It's okay. We'll link up for lunch, right?" Adeema asked, heading for the door.

"Right!" we said in unison. The Royal Elite Squad would have to conquer their days separately for now.

Kenzie

I made my way through the congested halls to Mr. DeWitt's Honors English class. He was the reason I was taking four Honors classes. He had always pushed me to be better than I thought I was, which was good and bad at times.

"Alejandra McKenzie Vega in the flesh!" a voice squealed from behind me with excitement and sarcasm lingering off her words. I turned around to see my crazy old friend Staci bopping down the hall. "I was starting to think you didn't love me anymore!"

"How could you say such a thing?" I asked, already knowing where this conversation was heading.

"Uh, well... you barely hang with the cheer squad like you used to. And me, for that matter anymore. You're always with those... *other girls*," she said, turning up her face in disgust as we walked into Mr. DeWitt's class.

"Don't do that! You know they are my friends too!" I said, giving her the eye as I took a seat.

"But I was your friend first!" she pouted.

"And no one can ever take that from you, Stace!" I said, squeezing her. Balancing different groups of friends was exhausting. Someone always felt neglected.

"You better be lucky I love you... *and* that I haven't found anyone that makes empanadas like your mother. Otherwise, I'd be gone."

Mr. DeWitt's baritone sounded throughout the classroom as he shut the door. "Alright, good morning, kings and queens. Let's get the day started." The class quieted down and awaited his instructions. "I'm so glad to see everyone getting back adjusted to Ridgewood. I see the wonder twins are back together," he said, looking at Staci and I. We put our fist up in the air in unison with a laugh as he flicked off the lights. "Let's kick off the class with current events. We are going to watch a news segment from this morning. Please pay attention because this will be tied into your morning writing. Cool?"

"Cooooool," the class yelled out in unison.

A news segment began playing on the TV screen. "Good morning, this is Brenda Day from FOX 5 Atlanta News," the anchor said.

"Really? Fox 5 though, Mr. DeWitt?" Ricky yelled out.

Mr. DeWitt had spoken out avidly against the one-sided nature of Fox 5 News, making the segment an odd choice for our class assignment. "Hey, it was the only link that wanted to download this morning," he said with a laugh. "Cut me some slack."

I put my head on the desk and watched the news flash across the screen as they discussed city rezonings, robberies, neighborhood gentrification and concerts coming to the area. It all was uninteresting until a story appeared on the screen that finally piqued my interest. "Last night, there was another fire in the metro Atlanta area—this time at East Point Mall," the anchor said. "There was a lot of damage and countless people were injured."

"Yo, I heard that fire was insane!" Staci said.

"I know... my friends were there." I replied

"But we weren't—oh, never mind. You're talking about the B-list friends." Staci rolled her eyes dramatically, but sensed my annoyance and changed her tone. "I'm sorry... are they okay?"

"Yes, they're fine. Thanks for the concern," I said sarcastically.

"Police are ruling the incident as arson," Brenda Day continued from the TV. "They also believe it's connected with the other local fires that have taken place over the past few weeks."

"Man, they need to find whoever is doing this ASAP!" Staci said. "Nowhere is safe! Now I can't even go to the mall... this is so tragic."

"Yeah, it's getting out of hand," Ricky said.

"Is there a hero amongst us that can put an end to this fiery terror?" Brenda Day asked before Mr. DeWitt switched off the TV.

"Okay class, I want you to write about whichever news segment stuck out to you. POV piece. Two pages, double-spaced."

The class quickly pulled out their pens, pencils, and notebooks to begin writing. My mind swarmed with potential ideas, but once my pencil hit the paper, the only thing that came out was ideas on how to catch the arsonist. We needed to extinguish this jerk *now*.

Adeema

"We're trending!" Libby Gray texted. I went to Twitter to check for myself. Lo and behold, Royal Elite Squad was number three on the trending lists. Atlanta was calling for us to come solve this fire fiasco. I was already focused on stopping this guy, so I was glad everyone was finally on board. It was time to get back in the game! He made it personal when he involved my friends.

"We need to meet after school," Kenzie texted the group. "I have a plan to end this!"

"I'm all in!" I responded. I sat back on the gym bleachers, ready for the day to be over, so we could get started on taking this guy down. There were only about fifteen minutes left in gym class. I had just dominated an intense game of dodgeball, and the guys didn't take losing to a girl too well. Now, they were all sulking in the corner of the gym. *I can't help there's a cannon in my left arm*, I thought to myself with a smirk,

"Ms. Hatem, let me talk to you for a second," Coach Smith said, adjusting his Falcons hat.

"Yes sir," I said, attempting to hide the phone that I wasn't supposed to have.

"You played an incredible game today and I've been noticing your ball skills have improved too."

It was surprising to hear, but it made me feel good to see that my talents were getting noticed. "Thank you, Coach! I've been really working hard. I come in before school to run drills and I even stay late some days," I said trying to contain my excitement.

"We'll be starting a summer basketball league this year and I'd love for you to try out. You got some skills—and I know Helga and the others would appreciate a great player like you on the team." Immediately, my excitement went away. *He just had to say her name.*

"Oh, uhm... well, I don't know" I stuttered, looking down at the ground.

"Well think about it, Hatem! I think you have some major skills," he said, raising his hand up to attempt a high-five.

"You know I can't—"

"I apologize. I almost forgot... but for real, think about it," he said before walking off. I wished I could have told him the reason my tone changed was because his team captain was the Ra's Al Ghul to my Batman. Or maybe the Kryptonite to my Superman would be a better description since every time she came around, I instantly got weak. I leaned back on the bleachers again and let out a long sigh. I really needed to get over my fear of Helga. She was coming between me and what I loved. I was probably the strongest girl at Ridgewood—maybe even the whole metro area—and I was scared of one middle school jerk. I was at a fork in the road internally. It was time to either stand up to Helga or I could end up in her shadow forever.

"What's up, gorgeous!" Libby Gray said, sitting down next to me, startling me half to death.

"Uh what are you doing here? Aren't you supposed to be in class?"

"See, I was... but then Ms. Chavez got snappy, saying graffiti wasn't real art even though, it clearly is," she fussed. "It's an expression, so how is that not art? I wasn't about to have anyone disrespect my fellow artists."

"She kicked you out of class, didn't she?"

"Yeah. I'm coming back from the assistant principal's office—thought I'd make a detour," she said, fiddling through her MK bag.

I leaned my head on her shoulder. "I'm glad you're here nonetheless."

"Rough class?" Libby Gray asked. "Is that girl still messing with you?"

"Huh? What girl?" I asked, acting as if I had no idea who she was talking about.

"Don't play coy with me!" Libby Gray said, linking her arm in mine. "They don't call me the social butterfly for nothing. I know everything going on at Ridgewood." I couldn't even bring myself to respond. "It's okay you don't have to say anything. Just let me know when you want me to handle it. I can ruin her if you want." It was the best feeling ever to know there was someone was in my corner. And for now, that was good enough for me.

Chapter 4

Janais

"Everyone rises, everyone falls. Everyone spends some nights alone!" I sang along to JoJo's music as I impatiently waited for my mother to pick me up from school. All my homework was already completed. The only thing left was to discuss DNA with my parents. Unfortunately, talking to my parents was about as much as fun as a paper-cut to the eye. They just didn't get me, especially lately.

"Hey Nay! You're still here?" Kenzie asked, sitting down on the bench next to me.

"You know it," I said, taking out my other earbud. "My parents are so busy, I swear they forget they have a child sometimes."

"Don't forget we're meeting my house tonight," Kenzie said as I nodded. "I have to jet to practice, but I'll see you tonight, okay? Cheer up buttercup!" She squeezed me tight like only a friend could. "And look who just pulled up?"

"Hey sweetheart. Sorry I'm late," my mom yelled from inside her new white Land Rover. I waved goodbye to Kenzie and headed to the car. *Maybe I can knock these questions out with*

Mom while we're in the car, so I won't have to do it later. I plopped down in the car and threw my bag in my back seat.

"Hey mom," I said, adjusting my seat so I could lean back.

"How was your first day back?" she asked, looking in the rearview mirror as she reapplied her lipstick.

"It was straight. It was cool being around my friends again." I pulled out my phone and decided to play Color Switch. I really wanted to put in my earbuds in and zone out, but I knew if I didn't get the assignment over with now, I'd be forced to talk with both of my parents once I got home.

"So, I have some homework in my science class and I have to ask you some questions. Is that okay?"

"Sure dear. I love helping you with your homework. Even though I haven't been able to in a long time. I think you're smarter than me."

She let out a laugh as I forced a smile and grabbed a notebook to write down her answers. "Okay, we're talking about genetics, DNA and what traits have been passed down to me." I scanned over my notes from class earlier and then at my mother who looked like she had just seen a ghost. "You okay?"

"Uhm, yes dear. Go ahead," she said, gripping the steering wheel tightly.

"Well, I just want to know what I may have gotten from you and Dad, and what may have come from Grandma Sharon, MiMi or Papa Ray." I pulled out my pen and waited for her to answer, so I could jot down the findings down—but she never spoke. I tried to snap her from the daze she was in. "Mom?" She continued to just sit there, facing forward with her hands at ten-and-two. "MOM!" I yelled.

"Yes... yes, Janais? I'm sorry... what did you say?"

"I asked about the family. Where do I get my rich complexion from? Do you think it's from Grandma Sharon's side or maybe Papa Ray's? And I know Aunt DaMaris is smart—do you think I get my love of knowledge from her?" I was starting to get even more curious about how I was made up. So many questions were dancing around my head, but sadly, not one had been answered yet. "Mom, what's going on? Are you okay?" I asked, growing concerned. Her hazel eyes were filled with puddles of water. I was so confused. *What did I do?*

"Your father and I really need to talk to you when he gets home, okay?" she said, fighting back tears.

"Ughhh, can't we finish this now?" I whined. "I have to meet with the girls later."

"No, this is important. Not another word." She mom turned up the radio to muffle her sniffles.

I turned over and looked out the window. I couldn't wrap my mind around what happened and why her mood changed so suddenly, but I didn't feel like getting yelled at anymore. I put my headphones in and closed my eyes. I guess the answers to all my questions would have to wait for another time.

Libby Gray

"STORM!!!" my father screamed as I walked in the door. I took a deep breath and proceeded to search the house in an attempt to find him. I used to love when he would call me Storm—but whenever I heard it nowadays, I wanted to run and hide. I still loved him dearly, but he hadn't been same since he came back home.

"Yes Poppa," I said, finally locating him laid out in the living room. He looked like he hadn't moved since I left this morning.

"Oh, there you are, my little Storm," he said, stumbling over his words. "You know... you know I love you, right? "

"I know," I said, looking into his green eyes that appeared glazed over. They didn't even shine anymore.

"I'm going to get it together for you, your brothers and your mom... *I promise.*" I knew he meant well, but I was over his empty promises.

"Don't make promises you can't keep!" CJ said, walking up behind me. My brother used to worship the ground Poppa walked on, but now, his tone was filled with such disdain. "Go do your homework, Libs."

"...Are you sure?" I whispered, tugging on my brother's arm. He looked at me and smiled. He was the spitting image of my father. I hugged him quickly and ran upstairs to my room. I slammed the door closed and threw myself on top of my giant bean bag. I screamed as loud as I could into my pillow, muffling my screams and hiding my tears. I turned around and let out the loudest sigh imaginable. My phone began to ring and I wanted nothing more than to use my abilities to go somewhere no one could find me and poof myself far away.

I looked down at my phone and saw it was my mom. My eyes instantly began to flow like a waterfall. *How did she know I needed her?* I didn't want to show her I was phased. I was the storm—I was supposed to rock the world, not have my world rocked. I ignored her call and laid on my side, squeezing my pillow tightly when a knock gently tapped on my door. "Yes!" I called out, quickly wiping my face.

"Sissy, it's me," my youngest brother Brice said sweetly. "Can I come in?"

"Come on in," I said, trying to act busy with work. Brice came to sit on the bean bag with me. I kissed his strawberry-blonde hair and we leaned back. "To what do I owe the pleasure?"

"Poppa and CJ were yelling again... and, well..."

"Don't worry, you can stay in here with me," I said, trying to deflect what he had overheard. "Wanna have a dance party like we used to?"

Brice hopped up. "Really? You're not too busy?"

"Too busy for my favorite younger brother? Never!"

He laughed. "I'm your *only* younger brother, Sissy!"

"Well, that means you win double time!" I joked, turning on my Bluetooth speaker. I began blasting our favorite song, "Thunder" by Imagine Dragons. We turned it up as loud as the Bluetooth would allow and danced from our wild manes to our tippy toes.

I was lightning before the thunder. "Thunder, feel the thunder. Lightning and the thunder!" Brice and I sang in unison. I picked him up and threw him on my bed. He laughed in such a therapeutically good way that warmed my heart to its core. Brice continued to jump on my bed while I danced on the floor with my hands in the air. The song came to an end and I joined Brice on the bed. He snuggled up to me.

"Thank you, Sissy" Brice said with a tight squeeze.

"Anytime," I said, hugging him back. I didn't need to be a superhero for Brice. I didn't even need to have it all together. He loved me just for being me.

Kenzie

My head bopped to the rhythm of "Havana," a song that always reminded me of family get-togethers on my Papa's side—lots of laughing, dancing and tons of good food like ropa vieja paired with rice and tamales, which were my favorite. Cubanos sure knew how to party and have a good time. The life of the party was none other than Abueltia Rose. She was my biggest fan in everything I did and always the first one on the dance floor. Thinking about my family was a short-lived distraction from the more pressing matters that were going on. I was so angry about our fiery foe that I couldn't even come up with a clever name for him besides the weird fire variations bouncing around my brain. *Flame Zane? Come on, what is that? A rollerblade brand?* I huffed and scratched another failed name out of my book. I looked up to see Libby Gray skipping her way over to me with her pigtails flapping in the wind.

"Hey there," Libby Gray said, plopping down next to me.

"Are you okay?" I laughed. "You normally enter a lot louder and later."

"Yeah, I am fine. I left early because I needed a break. But you know me, always good!" She forced a smile. I knew something was up because her dimples didn't show.

"Okay, I'll take your word for it. You ready to get back to business?" I asked, changing the subject.

"You have no idea! Every time I look in the mirror and see these second degree burns on my mid-section, I get even angrier," Libby Gray said, rubbing her belly.

"Don't stress Libs. We are going to get to the bottom of this!" I said, hoping I wasn't making a promise I couldn't keep.

"Kenzie! Libs! I think I got it!" Adeema yelled, running towards us.

"Looks like someone has news," Libby Gray said as we laughed in unison.

"Remember the first fire?" Adeema said, slapping her hands down on the table and breathing erratically. Even her usual perfectly-wrapped hijab was all over the place.

"*Respira, chicka!*" I laughed.

"English, Kenzie!" Libby Gray said, trying to see if Adeema was okay. "You see the woman can't breathe here!"

"*Respira* means 'breathe,' Libs," Janais said, startling us from behind.

"Nay! When did you get here?" Libby Gray asked.

"Just now. Got caught up with some home stuff and got lost in time."

"Focus y'all! I may have a lead!" Adeema said, finally catching her breath.

"Spill it!" I said, sensing her urgency. We all sat down around the park bench and awaited to hear what had Adeema so frazzled.

"Okay, we have to go back—"

"To the future!" Libby Gray interrupted with a laugh. " Sorry, I couldn't resist. As you were saying..."

We all simply shook our heads and smiled. "Like I was saying, we have to go back to the beginning... when the first fire happened," Adeema said, fiddling with her phone.

"When was that?" Janais asked.

Adeema turned her phone around and showed us a clip on her phone. "The I-85 bridge fire!" I exclaimed.

"That's right! That mission was intense. I am still fuming we didn't get any credit for that," Libby Gray said, rolling her eyes. "The news calling it a miracle was bogus. HELLOOOO! That was us! Four teenagers working together to keep the damage at a minimum."

"Wait, didn't the news blame that fire on a homeless person?" Janais asked, looking at the video.

"I've always found that hard to believe. I mean, come on... a homeless person caused a fire that required four super-powered girls to stop it?" I said. "Sounds like he was just the fall guy."

"That's what I was thinking too," Adeema said. "That fire

caused a city-wide havoc. People couldn't use I-85 for weeks. If someone was trying to rock the city, they definitely did."

"I just remember the traffic being awful," Janais said. "It would take my dad an extra two hours to get home."

"So, if it wasn't the homeless person, who is responsible?" Libby Gray asked. "And what does it have to do with the jerk who put me in the hospital?"

"That's exactly what I was thinking," I said. Those questions filled the air with concern but mostly silence. *What would compel someone to burn the bridge? What would someone really gain other than crazy traffic, angry people and one too many redirected roads?* "Wait... what if the fires were a distraction?"

"A distraction?" Adeema asked.

"From what?" Libby Gray chimed in.

"Look at these guys..." Janais said, flipping her tablet around to a map of some sort. "This represents the traffic flow before and after the explosion. 250,000 drivers were affected by that fire. Everyone had to be rerouted—and not just regular people like us... ambulances, police officers, jail transporters and servicemen all had to be diverted to different interstates."

"Wow, that's a lot of people," Libby Gray laughed. "I know those inmates weren't mad at the extra-long ride before getting locked back up again though. Had to be better than sitting in a cell!"

"Hey, I think you're onto something! What if that was the plan all along? What if they wanted those people to be diverted? Janais, did anything else major happen that day? I know it's probably hard to tell, but was there an increase in accidents or any other problems with those people being rerouted? I know roads had to be backed up."

"On it!" Janais said, scrolling on her tablet with super speed.

"Let me check the news for that day—I see one robbery, five accidents, a few other petty crimes... whoa, a patrol transport bus broke down and an inmate escaped."

"An inmate?" Adeema yelled.

"You're telling me we have real life criminals roaming the streets?" Libby Gray let out.

"What do you mean? We deal with real life criminals all the time."

"So, let's see," Janais said, scanning over the screen. "It looks like the vehicle that transports inmates broke down en route to another prison."

"Coincidence?" Adeema mumbled.

"I think not," Libby Gray said.

"An inmate by the name of Koa Tilo broke free," Janais said.

"Only one person escaped?" Libby Gray asked. "How did that manage to happen?"

"Janais—" I started.

"On it," she jumped in. "No, they haven't found him yet."

"Maybe it's all related to this Tilo guy? What does his rap sheet say?" Adeema inquired.

"Oh, I can do that one!" Libby Gray said. "I can dig up dirt on anyone. You should have seen the stuff I found out about—"

"Not now, Libs," I said, trying to keep her focused. "What can you tell us about Koa?"

"Okay, okay. Well, did you know 'Koa' means fighter? Pretty befitting, if you look at his record. He's been in and out of jail since he was our age. Larceny, grand theft auto, a few more robberies..." Libby Gray began reading off Tilo's crimes dating back further than before we were even born. Suddenly, she looked at us with fear in her eyes. "And homicide." This wouldn't be like our run-in with Yani. This man had no issue killing to get what he wanted. "This guy looks old though! Like Mrs. Jones old," Libby Gray said, looking defeated. "This can't be the guy we saw at the mall."

"Aside from some art awards in school, this guy was trash," Adeema said, looking at his transcript.

"But the person in the mall had abilities like us," Janais said. "He couldn't have been in the explosion at school with us."

"Libs, can you see if there is a connection between Tilo and Ridgewood? Maybe he or someone in his family went there. Or maybe, he used to work around there or something." Libby Gray got to work on her phone and tablet as I stood up and walked around. There had to be a connection between Tilo and this guy at the mall. *But what could it be?*

Adeema

The anticipation was killing me. I was just hoping and praying it wouldn't be another dead end. There wasn't much I could do at the moment other than wait. I twisted the tassels of my hijab, waiting for someone to speak up.

"I FOUND IT! " Libby Gray exclaimed. We had been waiting about 10 minutes for her to find some kind of connection between Tilo and the guy at the mall. "It was a little tricky at first, because the last names were different, and then, I had to go check out the hospital records to cross-examine the names. Sorry it took forever."

"It was only twelve minutes," I laughed, looking down at my watch.

Libby Gray rolled her eyes. "So this Tilo guy has never been married, but he's had a long on-again, off-again relationship with a young lady by the name of Roxanna. I found that out from her Facebook and Instagram. People really have to stop putting their whole lives on social media."

"But what would you do if you weren't connected to every-one's lives anymore?" Kenzie joked.

Libby Gray hesitated. "Hey, I guess you're right! Keep living out loud, people! But back to what I was saying... Roxanna and Tilo have three children together: Moani, Lahela and Keahi. Their last names are all Jackson after their mother."

"Pictures! Let's see pictures. What does the guy look like?" I said. I was ready to end this.

"Oh, he's hot!" Libby Gray said.

"Really Libs?" I said, confused. "This could be the guy who put you in the hospital and you're over here making googly eyes."

"Hey, cute is cute." She flipped her tablet around and showed us Keahi's Instagram page. "And guess what school Keahi and Lahela go to?"

"Wait, I've never seen this Keahi guy before," Kenzie said, getting a closer look at the guy who seemed to have a fascination with working out, football and fighting videos.

"Keahi actually goes to Ridgewood High!" Janais said. "I just looked in the database and his disciplinary sheet is just as long as his dad's."

"So, could this be our guy?" I asked. Libby Gray and Janais took their time looking over the photos.

"I can't really tell," Libby Gray said, throwing her head down on the table. "It was dark and he had a hood on."

Kenzie reassured her. "It's okay, we'll find him. We still have time."

"Uhm, actually..." Janais said in a voice that we knew all too well. Something was up.

She hit play on a video that had just gone live online. "Hello, this is Lucey Wilson with WSB Channel 11 news. Police have surrounded the Museum of Contemporary Art where a wild fire is currently in progress. "

"He's at it again!" Libby Gray exclaimed.

"What's up with this guy and art exhibits?" I asked.

Kenzie jumped up from the table with an epiphany. "That's it! The fires are the diversion! He has to be after the art! Think about it... if you steal the art and burn down the building, all the evidence is gone! It's the perfect cover!"

"Oh, he's smart!" Libby Gray said playing with her pigtails. "That's some evil genius type stuff."

"You can't date a supervillain, Miss Dawson!" I said, slamming my hands down on the table.

"I didn't even say anything," Libby Gray replied as we all looked at her and shook our heads.

"We have to go help!" Kenzie said, looking at us.

"But the Museum of Contemporary Art is all the way on the other side of town," I said. "How will we get there in time?"

Libby Gray stood up and waved her hands in the air before pointing at herself. "Uh, did y'all forget we have our own personalized transportation?"

"Ok. Everyone let's run home and get ready. We have a heist to stop," Kenzie said, grabbing her belongings from the table. "Let's meet on the corner of Summerwood & Oak ASAP." We all looked at each other one last time before jetting off in our different directions. I began running home. Nothing could describe this feeling. I was ready and determined. Now that we finally knew who we were looking for, he would be no match for us. This would be a breeze.

Chapter 5

Janais

I lived the farthest from Oak Park, but made it home quickly thanks to my lightning speed. I gathered myself before I tried to creep back in my house quietly, I really didn't have the energy to talk to my parents especially after my mom's weird breakdown in the car earlier. I inched up the stairs slowly, hoping they wouldn't betray me by making a sound.

I walked past my parents' room whose door happened to be cracked open and overheard my mom crying inside. "Paul, she knows! Our baby knows! I can't stand this. What have we done?"

"Breathe baby. It's going to be okay," my father responded. "We just have to tell her the truth, it's the only way." I froze mid-step. I knew eavesdropping was frowned upon, but if I was in trouble, I wanted a heads up. I stepped a little closer to get a better listen.

"She's going to hate me!" my mother cried. "Why did we wait so long? She's thirteen—almost a woman! We should have been told her she was adopted!"

My heart sunk to the depths of my soles. My ears rang as the hall began to spin. The wind had been knocked out of me. The word *adopted* ricocheted throughout my halls and back into my ears. *I have to get out of here.*

I rushed back to my room and shut my door quickly before they could notice I was home. I slid my body down the back of my door as I repeated the word over and over again. Each time I uttered it, my face was met by more and more tears. My stomach was in knots. *How could this happen?* They lied to me. My parents—or whoever they were—lied to me. *Where did I even come from? Who was I?*

I felt completely lost and confused. I made my way to the bathroom in an attempt to clean myself up. I stared at my reflection. I didn't know who I was anymore. The electricity surging through my body flashed through my veins at record-breaking speeds. My life flashed before my eyes—every encounter, every argument and every disappointment.

I hated them. I loathed them for making me believe a lie. My whole life, my whole existence was a lie. A part of me wanted to call the girls and tell them but they wouldn't understand—they all had loving families. I was in this alone.

I looked down at my phone. "Great, now I'm late," I mumbled, pushing my curls out of my face. If I didn't show in the next five minutes, they would know something was up. I thought about cancelling, but knew Libby Gray would pop over as soon as I sent the text.

I looked at myself in the mirror one last time. I could see the electricity zipping through my veins. I had to get out of this house. I quickly grabbed my suit from underneath my mattress, slicked my hair up into a bun and grabbed my boots. Suddenly, I didn't feel like crying anymore—I felt like knocking someone out. I needed an outlet before I exploded. Suddenly, I felt thankful that we had a mission and a bad guy who was about to receive all my rage. He wouldn't even know what hit him. I laughed manically, bouncing surges of energy back and forth between my hands. We had promised one another that we'd never kill anyone, but with the way I was feeling... who knew what would happen?

Libby Gray

I hid in the shadows of the alleyway of Summerwood & Oak. I was the first to arrive, so I began to stretch. I knew this fight wasn't going to be a breeze, so I wanted to prepare as much as I could. This guy didn't play any games, but little did he know, we were ready for whatever he could throw at us. If we worked together everything would be fine.

"Hey Libby!" Kenzie said, walking up to me. "You ready?"

"As ready as I'll ever be," I said confidently. "The last time he took us off guard. We won't make that mistake again."

"I hear you there!" Adeema said, walking up behind us.

"OMG! Okay, shoes!" I squealed, looking at her new navy-and-royal Airmax 90s.

Adeema looked down as if she'd forgotten what she had on. "Ooh these? They've been sitting in the box for months—thought I'd break them out finally."

"Wait, you've been hiding those and you continue to wear those ugly—"

"Hey, where's Nay?" Kenzie asked. We all looked at our phones to see if we had missed a text or call.

"Looks like she's meeting us there," I said, confused.

"Hmm, I guess. Libs, you ready? " Kenzie asked as we all linked arms.

"Where am I dropping us?" I asked.

"The service entrance," Kenzie said simply.

I gripped onto my two friends as tightly as I could and took a deep breath.

POOF I jumped us near the service entrance of the museum. It was getting easier and easier for me to do that. I could probably poof a car if I focused enough.

"Can someone call Nay?" Kenzie asked, adjusting her suit.

"No need—I'm here," she said, leaning against the service door with her arms folded.

"Where have you been?" I asked.

"Why are you worried about it?" she snapped back. "I'm here now." The old Janais was back. My eyes rolled so hard, they could have gotten stuck in the back of my head.

"I'm not even going to the address that," Kenzie said, trying to pivot the conversation she went on. "The first thing we need to do is to get all those people out safely. Then, and only then, can we go after you know who. Everybody got it?"

She put her hand in the middle of the circle. "Got it!" Adeema and I said, both putting our hands in the circle as well.

"Uh, Janais? Does that make sense?" Kenzie asked.

"Yeah whatever," she said, zapping the electrical keypad to gain access to the inside. We looked at each other and shrugged. Clearly, she had a plan of her own. We had no idea what was going on, but it wasn't the time nor place to be arguing. We followed Janais into the museum as alarms were going off everywhere. We weren't sure if it was because of what Janais had done or what was already in progress.

I was trying my hardest not to get distracted by the insanely talented works of art around us. I meanm we were creeping by Atlanta's best artists' work. "That's a Cosmo Whyte piece! Do you see that?" I said, geeking out. Janais rolled her eyes and brushed past me as if she were uninterested, which was weird since she was the one who originally put me on to his work. We were walking past greatness. I thought of Cosmo's previous work and remembered he put on an art show entitled "Starting A Bush Fire," which suddenly made things start to feel a little too real.

"Psst. Hey Nay, are you okay?" I asked, but she just ignored my question. Tensions were sky high and I only wanted this mission to be a success but the reality of the situation was quickly setting in. "Nay!" I said a little louder before grabbing her arm. She jerked away instantly and Adeema quickly pulled me back.

It was infuriating being ignored and I suppose Adeema felt that. "Breathe Libs, it'll be okay," Adeema said calmly. "The main hall where Keahi is reported to be is just up ahead. We need to focus." Janais' attitude was really beginning to irk me, but I was attempting to be the bigger person. We made it to the right wing of the museum where the fire was taking place. Flames danced around wildly as people screamed erratically. Chaos was happening and there was no time for teenage drama.

"Okay, Janais and Libs, see how many people need to be helped and get them out as quickly as possible," Kenzie instructed. "Adeema and I will try to get to the root of the fire."

"You all handle all that," Janais said, poised as if she were ready to zoom off. "I have something to take care of!"

With a flash, she was off into the fire. "Is she kidding me!?" I yelled out.

"We don't have time to figure it out. Libs, go help those people. We'll go try and find Nay and Keahi." Kenzie said before running off into the fire.

My blood was boiling. *How could Janais just leave us like that? Especially in the middle of a fight, where people were in danger?*

Kenzie was right though—we didn't have a lot of time to think about Janais and her ridiculous decisions.

I refocused and honed in on the screams and cries of the people trapped. "Help! Someone! Anyone! Help!" I heard someone's voice cry out. The cries of all the people together almost sounded melodious in a deathly terrifying way.

I leaned under the table to find the source of the first cries I could get to. "Grab my hand!" I didn't know who was going to be at the other end, but I knew they needed me.

"No, take my son first!" I heard a woman say between coughs, handing me a young boy who couldn't be more than two years old. I hadn't held a toddler since my younger brother was born and I was out of practice. "Go, take him! He's more important" the woman said coughing profusely.

"I can't leave you. You're coming too! " I said, grabbing the mother's arm. Before she could respond, I poofed her and her son outside the building where an ambulance, officers, and bystanders were waiting. The crowd erupted in amazement as I suddenly appeared in front of them.

"How did you—? Wait, you're one of those super girls! Thank you, thank you so much!" she said, hugging her son. I smiled and jumped back into the fire and continued to poof people outside. Men, women, children, and elderly. It was my mission to get them out.

Kenzie's voice came through my Bluetooth. "Libs, hurry up! We need you!"

"Copy," I said, heading back into the building. The fire was getting worse and it was making it almost impossible to breathe, let alone see. "Where are you all?" I asked, feeling lost and stumbling around the smoky building.

"We're by the Frida exhibit—east wing, near the gift shop,"

Kenzie said. "Hurry! We can't find Nay and the fire is getting worse" I maneuvered through the falling debris, piles of flames to my friends. "Here! Here! We're right here" Kenzie and Adeema said, grabbing me.

"Where's Nay?" I asked.

"We don't know," Adeema said, muffling her coughs. "What if something happened?"

We had to find her before it was too late.

Adeema

Five minutes had passed and there was still no sign of Janais. The longer we remained inside the museum, the smaller our chances of surviving became. The fire was growing more uncontrollable with each passing second. The building could collapse any moment and I wasn't sure if I was strong enough to hold it up.

"Shhh! I hear yelling," Libby Gray said, swatting her hand in front of Kenzie and I.

"But we weren't talking..." I said confused.

"Shhhh!" she said again, inching deeper into the museum. "It's coming from over there."

"I hear it now," Kenzie said.

"Where is it coming from?" I whispered.

Libby Gray pointed to a door that read STAFF ONLY. "I'll poof us inside" Libby Gray said linking her arms in ours.

"Be careful," I said. "I don't want to end up in a wall or anything."

"We should be alright... *I think*," Libby Gray joked.

"That's not reassuring at all," I mumbled.

"Let's go," Libby Gray said. Seconds later, we were on the other side of the door, standing between Janais and Keahi.

"You could have picked a better position, Libs!" I said, quickly getting into a fighting stance as Libby Gray and Kenzie followed suit.

"Get out the way!" Janais screeched. "This is my fight!"

"What are you talking about—we're here to help!" Kenzie said walking towards her.

"NO ONE ASKED FOR YOUR HELP!" Janais said, releasing electricity all around her. I ducked in just enough time to dodge a lightning bolt headed in my direction.

"This little one has a temper, doesn't she?" Keahi said, finally pulling his hood back from his face with a laugh, revealing his deep-waved curls that took over most of his face. "I am going to take a shot in the dark and assume this has nothing to do with me? What do you say, half-pint?" He stuffed a rolled-up painting in his duffle bag before throwing it over his back.

"You don't know me!" Janais yelled with tears in her eyes.

"Come on, Nay... we can take him!" Libby Gray said, inching towards her. "We have your back! We're family, remember?"

"I DON'T HAVE ANY FAMILY!" Janais screamed. She shoved past us with so much force and speed, we fell to the floor. When we looked up, we saw Janais had grabbed Keahi by his neck—she was squeezing so hard, the veins were protruding in her arms.

He just smiled and looked down at her. "To be so small, you all are incredibly annoying. All this talking and yelling... and don't get me started on this one who is in over her head. Does she not know I can end her life in an instant?" Kehai's eyes bounced between us and Janais, unfazed by her rage or even the fire wrapping around us. Suddenly, my dreams of being a hero didn't seem as fun as I hoped they'd be. "I've been entertaining Miss Georgia Power over here long enough, and now, the rest of you hop in here like annoying little Girl Scouts. I wasn't planning to kill anyone today, but I can very well make an exception!" he said, breaking free from her grasp and grabbing the collar of her shirt before lifting her high in the air.

Her little legs dangled as the fire around us grew almost instantly. "JANAIS!" we screamed out in unison.

Kenzie

I felt like I had caused a huge mess. What kind of person leads their team into a whirlwind like this with no way out? I had failed my team and I failed myself. We were helplessly watching Janais as she struggled to breathe, while we dwelled inside the tenth circle of hell. No ponytailed ideas could wiggle us out of this one.

Suddenly, a voice that sounded like Mrs. Jones said something inside my mind. "Miss Vega! Grab the girls and get out of there now!" I looked around and saw that she was nowhere to be found. *Great, now I am going crazy—I'm going to die a crazy person!*

"You're not crazy Miss Vega—it's Mrs. Jones. Now, grab the girls and leave out now! I can only stop time for so long."

I took a second to look around and saw everything frozen in place. *How did I not notice that the flames had stopped moving?* "But how did—?"

"Don't even *think* about asking another question," she said in an urgent tone. "GO!"

And just like that, time unfroze and Adeema began to shake me. "Kenzie, are you okay? We have to—"

"We gotta get out of here!" I yelled. "Now!" I grabbed Adeema and then Libby Gray's arm, so she could poof us out of the building.

"What about Janais?" Libby Gray said, looking concerned.

"Janais! Let's go!" I yelled. "We can handle it later!"

"NO, I CAN HANDLE THIS NOW!" Janais said creating a huge electrical ball above her head which only terrified me further. I knew that electricity and fire was never a good combination, no matter how you sliced it.

We have to get out of here! Libby Gray looked at me quickly and nodded, we both knew what had to be done. "Libby Gray, now!" I said, standing up. She ran towards Janais.

"Hey, what do you think you're doing?" Keahi asked, finally taking notice of the massive electrical current ensuing above his head. "Are you stupid? That's going to—"

"Try to flame your way out of this one!" Janais said, clapping her hands together into a loud sonic boom. Keahi let go of her to throw his hands up in an attempt to cover himself from all the electricity heading his way.

Libby Gray poofed midair and tackled her on the ground. "NOW!" I screamed as Libby Gray poofed Janais to us, and then returned us all back to Oak Park just as a humongous explosion erupted. We laid on the grass and collectively sighed. There was so much to talk about, but almost dying had been exhausting, so no one said anything. I covered my face with my arms and tried to fully comprehend what had taken place before taking my phone out my pocket and sticking my earbuds in one by one. I pushed play and Daniel Caesar's "Streetcar" began to soothe my anxiety.

Let me know

Do I still got time to grow?

Things ain't always set in stone

That be known let me know

I looked up at the sky. The clouds gradually entered my left eye and exited out of my right. The cool grass tickled the back of my legs. This would normally be where I would step up and say something to get the team back on track, but I was fresh out of encouragement.

"Life's just ain't fair...." I mouthed along with Daniel Caeser and heard talking, so I took out one of my earbuds.

"No. I'm not doing this!" Adeema said, sitting up. "I'm not acting like nothing happened! "

"I'm totally with you!" Libby Gray chimed in, standing up and staring at Janais who was still laying with her head in the grass and her face covered. "Janais, you have some explaining to do! And I dare you to try that Speedy Gonzalez crap—I'll be on your tail quicker than you can think!" Adeema stood as well and began pacing around, shadowboxing the air. Janais remained silent and Libby Gray looked at me. "Aren't you going to say something? You're the captain, leader or whatever. *LEAD*! Tell her we need answers!"

Libby Gray was upset and she had every right to be. "We all are upset. But what does yelling fix?" I said, trying to be the voice of reason and moving closer to Janais.

"And what exactly is fixed by ignoring the problem and sweeping it under the rug?" Adeema asked.

Libby Gray waved her arms around dramatically. "THANK YOU! At least one of y'all has some sense!"

I shook my head and began rubbing Janais' hair. "Are you okay?" I whispered to her.

"Is *she* okay—why don't you ask us if *we're* okay?" Libby Gray said. "We almost died because of her carelessness!"

"Libs, calm down. Maybe we just need to pray—" I began to say.

"PRAY! Are you kidding me, Kenz!" Libby Gray yelled, moving towards Janais. "She better bless these hands she's about to receive!"

I held my hand up used my abilities to freeze her in mid-air. "STOP IT! This is not what we're doing!"

"Come on Kenz, we aren't supposed to use our powers on each other!" Libby Gray cried as she remained suspended above my head. "I have no problem with you. I'm just tired of this!"

"Look, I'm sorry, okay?" Janais said, leaning up with her face stained with tears. "I don't know what's wrong with me." We all looked at her, wondering what she would say next. She sat up and tried to wipe her face with her sleeve. "Y'all just wouldn't understand!"

"Try us!" Adeema said.

Janais looked over our faces and took a huge deep breath. "Okay, so this is what is going on..."

Adeema

We stood there dumbfounded. *Adopted.* I couldn't imagine how I would feel if I heard that word come out of umi's mouth.

"*Lo siento,*" Kenzie said, hugging Janais who started crying on her shoulder.

"It's just been a lot," Janais said in-between sniffles. "I don't know who I am anymore. Where did I even come from?"

I sat down next to her as Libby Gray continued to stand, staring at us. She didn't seem as shaken by the news. "That still doesn't excuse your bratty attitude!" she said, folding her arms.

"LIBS!" Kenzie and I let out in unison.

"What?" Libby Gray said, shrugging her shoulders. "Y'all were thinking it too, shoot."

"She's right," Janais said. "I've been off for some weeks now. This adoption stuff was new. It isn't an excuse at all."

"We are all going through our own demons, Nay," Kenzie said, reassuring her. "You don't have to worry about that. You are not alone! We are here, contrary to what you might feel."

"I can definitely attest to that," I said, thinking on all I had encountered. "I've been going back and forth on if I want to wear my hijab anymore."

"What? Why?" Libby Gray asked, finally joining the rest of us.

"I... I don't know. It's just the climate of the world. I still want to practice Islam—it's a part of who I am. But y'all don't understand how it is to be judged the instant someone sees you."

"Uh, I'm Black," Janais said, scrunching up her face.

"Latina!" Kenzie said with a wave of her hand.

"FAT," Libby Gray said jiggling her belly.

We all looked at each other and erupted in euphoric laughter—the stomach-cramping, rolling-on-the-floor, barely-able-to-speak type of laughter. It was crazy how much we had in common, even through our differences. We all laid back on the grass and grabbed hands, beginning to look up at the passing clouds.

"Libs, I'm so sorry," Janais said suddenly. "I've been treating you so—"

"Nay, I love you!" Libby Gray interrupted. "Just don't cut me off like that again!"

"PRAISE GOD! They finally made up!" Kenzie said, waving her hands in the air, just as an alert went off on all our phones, pausing our happy moment. It was from Twitter—we were getting tagged like crazy.

Libby Gray sat up excitedly. She was all about social media, so it had to be a dream for her. "Do y'all see this? Royal Elite Squad is trending!"

"We're number one?" I asked in amazement. We had never been that high before.

"Everyone must be thanking us for saving the Museum of Contemporary Art!"

"Uhm, let's not get too excited. Look at what they are saying about us," Kenzie said, showing me a tweet by a woman calling us monsters.

"Twitter is full of trolls. That's probably just one person," Libby Gray said, scrolling on her phone vigorously. "They can't all be bad, right?"

"Oh my God," Janais blurted out with her mouth wide open.

"That's not good, is it?" I asked.

"Look what Channel 2 News said," she answered, watching a video on her phone. Her face let me know it was probably bad news.

I headed over to their Twitter account and couldn't believe my eyes. "Wait, they're blaming *us* for the building collapsing?" Kenzie yelled out. "That doesn't make any sense—Keahi was the one flaming around!"

"So, the pyromaniac gets off and the real heroes become the villains?" Libby Gray snapped. "Are you kidding me?" I looked at all the things people were calling us: freaks, science experiments gone wrong, terrorists, and many other things I wouldn't dare let escape my mouth.

"Look at this!" Libby Gray said, showing us a tweet from Georgia Power saying they were trying to restore power back to all the residents without it. "It looks like Janais knocked out all the power on the Fulton County grid—I didn't even know you could do all that!"

"Now that you mention it, you were kicking out some real official electrical-based powers back there," I said, forcing a laugh. "Who knew you were that strong?"

"I didn't know either to be honest," Janais said, shrugging her shoulders. "It felt like the madder I got, the stronger I became." I started to wonder if all our abilities would react the same way if we got angry as well.

"So, what are we going to do about this?" Libby Gray asked frantically. "We can't continue to let them say these kinds of things about us. Our reputations are at stake!"

"Technically, they don't know it's us," Janais said with a laugh.

"Oh, you know what I mean. What do you think, Kenz?" she asked as Kenzie was putting her hair up into a ponytail.

"Go home, get some rest. First thing after school tomorrow, we're finding this fiery demon. We have to show the world who is really responsible for all this havoc."

I laughed. "Fiery demon? We might as well call him the Under Lord."

"Nah, that doesn't have a great ring to it," Libby Gray said.

"What about Under King?" Kenzie suggested.

"That's it!" we said in unison.

"Under King is going down tomorrow!" Kenzie said as we all turned to head home in our separate ways. "We'll be rested, ready and fighting as a team this time!"

Chapter 6

Janais

Releasing some of the feelings and emotions I had been harboring was so liberating. I felt lighter. But in the grand scheme of things, telling my friends was probably going to be way simpler than confronting my parents. I stopped to get ice cream on the way home from Bruster's. I needed some comfort food before I braced the unknown conditions of my household. I crept open my red-stained front door and inched inside. I looked around and saw no one in the foyer or the living room.

"Hello?" I called out, unsure if I really wanted a response. I still didn't know what I going to say to them. I didn't even have the words to properly explain what I was feeling. My whole life had been turned upside down. It was bad enough I was going through regular teenage changes—now I had to deal with this too.

"Janais! Baby, is that you?" my mom asked, running down the stairs. She wiped her face quickly, trying to mask the fact she had been crying, but there was no hiding the tear stains on her cheeks and the redness in her eyes. I stared at the woman I had spent the past thirteen years calling mom and felt my heart being ripped into pieces with each step she took, even though I tried to stand tall and not let her see I was so hurt.

"Hey, baby girl," my dad said, coming out of his office and walking closer to me. "We're so glad you're home. Is everything okay?" We all stood in the living room looking at one another. We were all waiting for someone else to speak. The song in my earbuds changed to "When I Grow Up" by Nicole C Mullen, a childhood favorite. I remembered singing it with my parents when I was little, wanting to be just like them. But now, as I looked at them, I wasn't sure who was looking back at me.

"Baby, we need to talk," my mom said, motioning me to sit on the couch. She sat down on the floor in front of me and ran her hands over my face and through my wild curls before trying to speak. "First and foremost, your father and I want you to know that we love you so much. You're undeniably the best thing that has ever happened to us."

She placed her hand on my knee and my leg began shaking nervously. I bit my lip tightly. *Don't cry, Nay. Don't cry.*

"Your mom is right!" my dad said, sitting down next to me and rubbing my hair. "Everything we do is for you." The temperature in the room seemed to be increasing and decreasing simultaneously. They looked at each other nervously and I started to wish they would hurry up before I passed out from anticipation.

"There's no easy way to say this," my mother said, barely able to make eye contact with me. "I've been practicing for years and it never came out right." My father grabbed her hand and I felt my eyes beginning to water. "Remember when we told you Mommy had ovarian cancer many years ago and beat it? Well, that period of my life was filled with so much pain. I suffered from a lot in my early twenties, but when I got older, it got even worse. I ended up developing a tumor in my ovaries. After chemotherapy, surgery, and medicine, I was able to overcome... but it cost me something major." She was in full meltdown mode at this point. She was normally so well put together, I could hardly recognize her now. "And the doctors... they told me I would never be able to have a child, because of all the damage it caused."

"It broke our hearts to hear that," my dad interjected. "Your mother and I wanted nothing more than to be parents and have a family of our own. We dreamed about you! With the doctors' help, we weighed our options. Adoption seemed like the best option for us. And it was a long process, but as soon as they sent us a picture of a beautifully brown, curly-headed two-month-old, we knew..."

"I've been dreaming about that little face for as long as I could remember," my mom said, grabbing my hands. "Far before I actually saw you. The picture confirmed you were our child. You were our baby. Blood couldn't make you more mine."

"So, you're not my real parents?" I stuttered out through hot tears. It was the only question I could manage to form. It was one thing overhearing it the first time. This time hit deeper in ways unimaginable. I just wanted it to be a terrible joke.

"Baby no—we're your real parents!" she pleaded. "We were at your first doctor's appointment. Saw you take your first steps. Heard your first words. Everything. You're *ours*." I didn't even know what to say. I understood their reasons why, but I just wanted to go to my room and process it all before my emotions forced me to do something crazy like electrocute the entire house.

"Your mother is right. We love you! That's all that matters

right now."

"I don't think so," I said, making a dash to my room. "It's not enough!"

"JANAIS—" my mother yelled out.

"It's okay," he answered. "Let her go."

I slammed my door and jumped in bed. All I wanted to do was cry in my bedroom.

Alone.

Kenzie

"*Lavantate y brilla!*" I heard my mother yell from outside my room.

"*Si, mama!*" I yelled back, using the hair diffuser to dry my hair. I wasn't going to chance letting it air dry. Little did she know I had been up since five A.M. trying to get the smell of ash and smoke out of my hair. Three wash-and-conditions later, and it still felt like I was sitting in the middle of an inferno. Shockingly, I had slept well the night before after we talked Janais down. She videocalled us. Our girl was truly going through it, but we were there for her through it all.

I grabbed my Ravens windbreaker, a tanktop and a pair of shorts. I laced up my sneakers as I watched my bookbag pack itself while my hair put itself in a ponytail with a nice French braid. Having abilities sure came in handy when it was time to get ready and I was getting really good at controlling things in my room these days. An alert on my phone reminded me the bus would be arriving in five minutes, forcing me to snatch my bookbag out of the air before grabbing my trumpet and cheer bag.

As I waited in front of my house for the yellow chariot to

escort me to school, I was surprised to see Adeema running up to me, which was odd because she lived in a completely different neighborhood.

"Uh, good morning?" I said confused.

"I know you're wondering why I'm here," Adeema said, adjusting her jogger pants and Nikes. "I just wanted to ride the bus with my friend. You know... see if you did Ms. Gilmore's homework. "

"You already know I don't have Ms. Gilmore—I am in AP English with Mr. DeWitt. But you knew that," I said, pulling her closer. "Why are you *really* here? Not that I mind, but I'd rather not be lied to."

Adeema fidgeted with the zipper on her jacket. "Fine, I just didn't feel like riding my bus to school."

"It's that Helga girl, isn't it?" I asked, causing Adeema to looked at me surprised. "Libs told me! You should stand up to her! Or at least let Libby beat her tail like she's dying to do anyway." We both laughed as we got on the bus, waving to the driver Mr. Bryson and sitting down near the middle of the bus.

"I know I need to do something, but I'm stuck right now. If I do anything to her, she's going to see me as some violent Muslim girl that she probably already assumes I am anyway. If I do nothing, I'm just a coward," Adeema said, leaning against the window. I knew she was right, but it was tough feeling held responsible by every decision that every person in my race and religion had made. Especially when all I was trying to do was just live.

"Well I know right now it seems impossible, but you'll figure it out. Just don't kill her," I giggled. "I don't think it's a good look for a hero." We continued in idle conversation the rest of the way to school. There were few moments in life where I felt like a normal teenager, but this was one of them. It felt good just chopping it up with my girl about random things like TV, drama at Ridgewood and the occasional boy. For that quick ten-minute ride we didn't discuss being heroes, villains, powers or anything. We just laughed which was so needed in the midst of this mess.

We hopped off the bus and made our way towards the building. "I wonder where Libby Gray and Janais are?" Adeema asked, walking inside.

"HEYYYYY!" Libby Gray yelled from down the hall.

"Found her," I laughed, putting in my locker combination.

"How are my girls doing?" Libby Gray asked, checking out her reflection in her locker mirror.

"Someone is chipper today!" I laughed, stuffing items inside my locker.

"Thanks to some good sleep and a burst of creative energy, I'm feeling superb" Libby Gray said, flipping her curls around.

"Hey guys," Janais said walking up to us. Her curls were perfectly sculpted into a high poof on top of her head, making her look like a beautiful pineapple.

"How's my favorite *fine-apple* doing?" I asked.

She only shrugged her shoulders and forced a smile. "I am just happy to be at school. It is a pleasant distraction from my terrible life. I really hope we're not talking about genetics today—I really can't stomach learning about how many more ways I'm not related to my parents." We knew it was going to take time until she got back to her normal self. I was just glad we were all on the same page. I hoped it would make catching Under King easier this time.

We had almost made it to Mrs. Jones classroom when a basketball came flying out of nowhere and smacked Adeema in the back of her head. We turned around to see Helga standing there, laughing hysterically. "My bad. Didn't see you there. It's almost like you weren't even there. Like you were invisible."

"Adeema, I swear... let me get her!" Libby Gray said, balling up her fists as Janais and I did the same.

"Just say the word," I joined in. Adeema simply picked up the ball that rolled on the ground and remained quiet. I had never seen her so upset. I didn't know what was about to happen, but knew it wouldn't be pretty.

"Didn't see you on the bus today, *Muhammed*! You're not hiding from me, are you?" she asked, high-fiving her lackeys. Adeema didn't respond, only squeezing the basketball tighter and tighter. "Why don't you go ahead and throw the ball back now, huh? You can do that, can't you?" Adeema still refused to speak. "Come on, Osama! It's easy. Probably as easy for you as building a bomb."

Before Helga could finish laughing, Adeema threw the basket-ball at her with so much force, it knocked her into the lockers. Helga slid down the lockers in defeat. The halls instantly got so quiet you could only hear the AC unit running. It didn't last long as an eruption of laughter took off with Libby Gray's loud mouth igniting the flame. Adeema, however, still looked as serious as ever. I linked her arm in mine and guided her into Mrs. Jones class.

"Y'all give me a second!" Libby Gray said, laughing as she walked up to Helga and began making a video on Snapchat. "I need a picture of this!"

"Come on, Libs," Janais laughed, trying to get her inside the class before the bell rang.

"Hey, Helga! You got knocked the—"

"LIBS!"

"Fine, fine I'm coming," Libby Gray said, putting her phone

away and leaning over to Helga. "If you ever mess with my friend again, you're going to have to deal with me. And I promise you it'll be way worse than a basketball." She skipped up to us and we entered Mrs. Jones class just as the bell sounded. All I could do was laugh. *Just when I thought my life was normal.*

Libby Gray

"Come on, come on," I mumbled, tapping my pen against the desk. There were only fifteen minutes left before the day was done. My mind was focused on everything but Mr. DeWitt's rant on the president's leadership abilities and the importance of voting. My eyes jumped back and forth between the wall clock, my phone and my watch, hoping that time would speed up somehow if I looked at all of them repeatedly.

"Ms. Dawson," Mr. DeWitt let out, silencing the quiet whispers of the class.

"Uh, yes sir!" I said, pretending to focus as he sat on his desk and cut his eyes at me through his wide-frame glasses.

"Am I boring you?" he asked.

"Boring is a relative term, sir," I said, trying my best to deflect the question.

"Relative, huh? Well, how about you come to the front of the class and talk about something that interests you. Anything goes," he said, readjusting his wide frames. "The last fifteen minutes are all yours." I really hated when teachers did this to prove a point. The class began to stare at me and I sat there for a second, trying to figure out what I was going to talk about. I couldn't talk about being a part-time hero or how we were going to try to capture a flame-throwing villain we nicknamed Under King. I definitely didn't feel like rehashing the depressing nature of everything going on at home. I was drawing a complete blank. Mr. DeWitt refused to let me off the hook, continue to stare at me as if an idea was going to magically going to appear in thin air.

"Oh, Mr. DeWitt I have a question!" I voice blurted out from behind me. I looked over to see Yani raising her hand. She looked at me and nodded. We hadn't really spoken much since our major encounter last year. Either way, I appreciated the distraction.

"What's that?" Mr. DeWitt asked as Yani began to twist her purple faux locs.

"Well, I was curious on how you got involved in music? We know that is your first love. When did you fall in love with it?" His face lit up like a Christmas tree as he hopped up from his desk and headed to his laptop, proceeding to play us all these different artists from over the years. I looked at Yani, who gave me a slick smirk and went back to scrolling on her phone. *Who would have thought our old nemesis would look out for me?*

I went back to scrolling through my phone and messaging the girls.

Kenzie: My clothes still smell like an ash tray
Adeema: You too? I washed my hijab like 5 x's and it still smells
Janais: I finally got the smell out of my hair which took forever.

I was about to tell the girls I was working on new suits for us to wear, but I stopped mid-text when I heard the class laughing. I looked up to see Mr. DeWitt bopping around the classroom, singing along with the song he was playing.

"What do y'all know about this!" he said, nodding his head and tapping his hands on the podium to the beat. "Sam Cooke's *Chain Gang*. This is a classic! Doesn't get much better than this!"

A few students got up and started dancing—before I knew it,

everyone was up, trying to catch the rhythm with Mr. DeWitt. Everyone began egging me on as I showed off my moves in the middle of the class. I had almost forgotten how much I loved to dance. To their amazement, I did a pique turn into an arabesque. I hadn't taken ballet since I moved to Atlanta two years ago, but obviously something had stuck with me. I could tell that my peers were amazed that I could dance so well. I was showing out and the attention was giving me all the life I needed. Suddenly, the bell rang and Mr. DeWitt dismissed us to go home.

I gathered my belongings, just as Yani came up behind me. "So, you can really dance, I see." I turned to see her playing a video of me dancing on Snapchat.

I nodded and smiled. "Thanks... and thanks for earlier too," I said, grabbing my purse and walking to the door. "You know how Mr. DeWitt can be."

"Yeah, he's cool and all, but sometimes he does the most," Yani said, walking with me. A few months ago, we were fighting each other in these very halls, but it was a new year, so I would let it slide for now.

The halls flooded with people rushing to the bus lane, after school activities and everywhere else in-between as we talked about the homework assignment I didn't know we had. I saw the girls walking towards me and their faces said it all.

"Uh, hi you two," Adeema said, eyeballing us.

"What's good y'all?" Yani said. "What's up, Kenzie?"

"Hey Yani," Kenzie said, squinting her eyes. "Haven't seen you much lately."

"I've been laying low, ya know?" Yani said, playing in her hair yet again.

"Staying out of trouble, we hope," Adeema said, folding her arms as Kenzie elbowed her in the side.

Yani snickered and rolled her eyes. "Sooo... yeaaaaaahhhh... I'mma catch y'all later. We'll talk about that homework assignment later tonight, Libby Gray," she said before walking off into the crowd.

The girls' eyes followed her until she was blended in with everyone else, before they turned back to look at me. "Look, I know what y'all are going to say!" I said, throwing my hands in the air. "But it's not what it looks like."

"Isn't she the enemy?" Adeema asked incredulously.

"Man, come on... don't do that," I said.

"Technically, she redeemed herself at the end, didn't she?" Janais said as we walked to the carpool lane.

"Right! Plus, Kenzie was the one who told her who we were anyways," I said, trying to deflect.

"No, no... don't change the subject like that," Kenzie said. "It's just weird that y'all were talking. *We* don't even talk anymore. She quit the cheer team too."

"I still don't care for the girl, that's all" Adeema said, folding her arms.

"As much as she got on my nerves with all that weather mess last year, I'd much rather have her on my side than against," I whispered. Maybe it was time to finally forgive Yani and let bygones be bygones.

Adeema

We decided to meet at Janais' crib since her house was one of the few that didn't have a ton of people crawling around. The girls and I sat in Janais' room. Homework came first, Kenzie's rules. She insisted that if we were going to do this hero thing, we had to keep our grades up.

Luckily, I didn't have any, so I laid across Janais' bed and tossed my basketball in the air. Libby Gray was rehearsing her lines for drama class in the corner, Janais was writing a paper on the Trans-Atlantic slave trade while Kenzie was laying on the floor, doing math that had way too many numbers and letters in it for my liking.

I wished they would hurry up, so we could get to the real reason we were there: we had to clear our names. Twitter was still slinging us through the mud, and even the news had gotten in on us, calling us science experiments gone wrong.

"Can't you toss that ball a little quieter?" Libby Gray snapped. "Some of us are trying to focus here!"

I laughed before throwing the ball in the air one more time for good merit, making sure to smack the ball loudly when I caught it. "Better?" I asked with a smile.

Libby Gray threw down her script and stood in the middle of the room. "I can't think with She-Hulk over here causing all this ruckus, so can we go ahead and work on finding Under King?"

"I can finish my paper in the morning," Janais said, closing her textbook. "It's only a thousand-word essay."

"A thousand words? How can you write that much?" Libby Gray asked.

"Your Twitter page has over 2,000 tweets—what are you talking about?" I said, sitting up.

"That's different…" Libby Gray said, rolling her eyes.

"Okay, fine. Let's get started," Kenzie said, putting her belongings in her bag. She pulled her hair up into a ponytail on top of her head. "Okay, what do we know?"

"Well, I can say what we *don't* know," I said, sitting on the floor with the other girls. "We don't have any evidence that Under King is even still alive. He could have quite possibly died in that explosion."

"Libs, can you check it out?" Kenzie asked. Libby Gray pulled out her laptop and phone, beginning to scroll like a mad woman. "Janais, can you see if anymore fires have taken place? I know it was just yesterday, but we need to make sure." Janais got on her laptop as Kenzie looked at me. "Now, we just have to figure out a way to stop him if we actually get him."

"Too bad none of us have water powers," I laughed. "We could just hose him down."

The look that Kenzie gave me let me know she didn't appreciate my humor, but it changed quickly as she hopped up. "Wait a minute..."

"Found something!" Libby Gray said. "Looks like he is still active on Instagram and Facebook. Ugh, who uses Facebook anymore?"

"Old people," Janais laughed from behind her computer.

"So, he's a sophomore at Ridgewood High and plays safety for the football team... or at least he used to before he got kicked off the team. He was born on January 11th..." Libby Gray started to read off everything she could find about Under King's as if it were a novel.

"I'm surprised you didn't find his social too," Kenzie laughed.

"Wait, do you need it? Because I'm almost sure I can get it..."

"Nooo. You did good though," Kenzie said. "But y'all listen to this. We all know what a disaster it was going up against Under King last time—we may need help this round."

"What are we going to do? Ask Mrs. Jones?" I laughed at the thought.

"Oh, that would be funny," Libby Gray said, giving me a high-five.

"I was thinking someone a little younger," Kenzie said with a smirk.

"But who do we know that could help?" Janais asked with the same confused look Libby Gray and I shared.

"We know one other person with powers," Kenzie said as her smile grew even bigger.

"You better not say who I think you're going to say…" I said, giving her a look.

"Look, I know it's a long shot… but she could help us beat Under King!" Kenzie said with her hands on her hips. We all sat there in shock. She had to be kidding.

Chapter 7

Janais

I stuffed my mouth with Mike & Ikes as I watched Kenzie and Adeema make a list of pros and cons. The subject: *If Yani Should Join RES to Defeat Under King.* Adeema and Kenzie were both adamant about making their points. I didn't care either way—as long as the job got done, I was with it.

"My money is on Adeema!" Libby Gray said, pulling up a chair up next to mine.

"I don't know," I said, giggling with Libby Gray. "Kenzie has some heat in her."

"It just doesn't make sense why you would want her on our team," Adeema said, clapping her hands together. "She's already showed us what kind of person she is."

Kenzie put her hands on her hips. "Come on now! We all make mistakes and she made one. Plus, she's been squeaky clean since!"

"That we know of," Adeema said, rolling her eyes and turning away from Kenzie. Kenzie mumbled something in Spanish so quickly that I could barely keep up. What I did make out was something that would get me slapped in my mouth if my mom heard me say them.

"Oh, I can do that too!" Adeema said, beginning to speak in Arabic. Libby Gray and I looked at each other and began laughing. We laughed so hard we fell out of our seats.

"What's so funny?" Kenzie and Adeema asked in unison.

"Y'all are!" Libby Gray said.

"Is this how we were a few days ago?" I asked, wiping a tear out of my eye from laughter. "If so, I'm so sorry. This is comical." Kenzie and Adeema did not seem amused at all.

"Look it's simple. You both are correct," Libby Gray said. "There are pros and cons to letting Yani help us."

"But in the end, we do have to think about the greater good," I said. "If there is even a small possibility she can help, don't you think we need to take it?"

"Okay, fine! But I'll be keeping a close eye on her!" Adeema said throwing herself on my beanbag chair.

KNOCK KNOCK

My mother peeked her head in from behind the door and my disposition quickly changed.

"Hey ladies. I didn't know you all were here. I can order everyone some take out from that Chinese restaurant Janais loves if you all are hungry?" my mother said, obviously trying to butter me up. Stixx was my favorite.

"That sounds good. Can we get some lo mein!" Libby Gray exclaimed.

"Anything without pork works for me!" Adeema added.

"I've been craving egg drop soup if I'm being honest," Kenzie said while I remained quiet.

"What about you, baby girl?" mom asked.

"I'm okay," I lied. My stomach growled in protest, knowing I wanted something to eat. Especially from Stixx.

"Oh, okay. Well, I'll get your favorite anyway, just in case you want to eat it later." I felt her eyes staring through the side of my face, but I refused to budge. I didn't have anything to say to her even if my stomach disagreed.

"Thank you, Mrs. Wright," the girls said in unison. My mother shut the door, leaving the attention on me.

"What's up Elsa? The cold front is still going on?" Libby Gray asked, nudging my side.

"I don't know what I'm supposed to say," I said, avoiding eye contact with everyone.

"Look, we aren't arguing that your parents should have told you years ago! That's a fact!" Adeema said.

"But they are still your parents," Kenzie said. "They raised you. They have been there since the beginning. There are a million pictures of you over the past thirteen years. You can't say they weren't there."

I folded my face up and fought back the urge to cry. I knew they were right, but it didn't hurt any less. I didn't feel like dealing with it at the moment.

"So let's get back on task... ehat are we about to do?" I asked, shaking myself off as the girls stared blankly. "Fine, I'll figure out a plan on my own. Libs, text Yani to see if she can come over. We are talking about trying to recruit her and we haven't even asked her yet." I sat up, doing my best to act unfazed.

Libby Gray looked at Adeema and Kenzie, who simply shrugged her shoulders. "Okay, I guess I'll get on that now," Libby Gray said as the girls turned to busy themselves.

My problems needed to be addressed one day, but today, it could wait.

Kenzie

We sat around the dinner table, eating Chinese food and waiting for the doorbell to ring. Surprisingly, Yani had agreed to come over to talk. We thought it best to tell her the plan in person instead of a direct message.

"Can you pass me an egg roll?" Janais asked.

"This is like your third one," I said with a laugh, passing them her way.

"I'm a stress eater," she snapped before grabbing them out of my hand. "Thankfully, I have a high metabolism. If I didn't, I'd be as big as—"

Libby Gray stabbed her fork into her lo mein, cutting her off. "As big as what, Nay? As big as what!"

"Never mind," Janais laughed.

"Mmmhmm, I thought so."

"Is everyone enjoying everything okay?" Mrs. Wright asked, fluffing her curls in the kitchen mirror. She was dressed to impress as always, wearing a black strapless gown that kissed the ground when she walked. Ruby red matte was on her lips and her cheeks looked as if they were highlighted in gold. We nodded in unison. "I'm glad. Mr. Wright and I have a gala to attend this evening. You girls are more than welcome to spend the night if your parents allow it. I'm sure Janais would love the company." Mrs. Wright kissed Janais' cheek and told her she loved her before giving us a smile and heading to the garage.

DING DONG

We all stopped eating and looked at each other. She was here.

"So who's going to get the door?" Adeema asked.

"It's Nay's house," Libby Gray said, smiling hard in her direction.

"Fine!" Janais said, wiping her mouth.

"I'll go with you," I offered.

We both walked towards the door as the doorbell rang again. "I'm coming!" Janais hollered. We took a breath and opened the door. Yani stood there twisting her purple faux locs and blowing a bubble with her gum. "Hey Yani, come on in," Janais said. I followed behind as she closed the door. Tensions were high, but everyone was putting up a good front.

"What's up!" Yani said, nodding her head at the girls. If looks could kill, Yani would be dead-on-sight thanks to Adeema. "Is it good?" Yani asked Libby Gray, who was still stuffing her mouth.

Libby Gray quickly swallowed and smiled "Girl, yes! Do you want some? Janais' mom bought way too much. We have more than enough."

"Are you sure?" she asked

"Yes, we insist!" Janais said, pulling up a chair for her to sit. I handed her a plate and we all sat around the table, watching her grab a little bit of everything. She bowed her head for a quick prayer and began eating. No one spoke. Yani looked around the table and we looked away quickly, so it wouldn't seem so awkward.

"Okay," Yani said, wiping her mouth. "I know y'all didn't invite me over here to stare at me and eat Chinese food. What shakes?"

"What shakes, huh?" Janais repeated, nudging Libby Gray. "Yeah, you're right... we didn't invite you over here for the Chinese. "

"Yeah, no—we have something to ask you," Libby Gray said, forcing a smile. "Actually, Kenzie is going to ask."

Everyone looked at me and I took a deep breath. "Well, we actually want to ask you a favor."

"A favor?" she said with a side eye. "I didn't think we were still cool enough for those, Kenz."

"Look, chill!" Adeema snapped. "Don't start with the attitude!"

Yani jerked her head around to Adeema. "First of all, no one was talking to your brolic-looking self anyways—I was talking to Kenz. I'm trying to be nice, but don't test me."

Janais and Libby Gray tried to mask their laughs. "Look Yani, we didn't ask you here to fight," I said, trying to bring the conversation back. "Oddly enough we're on the same side. We need your help defeating a new villain."

"I know you're not talking about any of that crime-fighting garbage. Heroism is y'all's M.O., not mine."

"So, you have been acting like a villain!" Adeema said

"What I've been doing is minding my own business—why don't you try it!" Yani said.

I gave Adeema a look, telling her to shut up. "Man, whatever... you all handle this!" Adeema said, storming off and leaving us looking at each other.

"Look, we appreciate you keeping our secret over all these months... that's major," Janais said.

"Wasn't my secret to tell," Yani said. "But I still don't know what I could possibly do for y'all. And what's so powerful that y'all four can't stop it? Even though, now that I think about it, I had your number too until I got sucker-punched from behind by the big one!"

"Yeah! We get it! You're powerful too. That was just one fight though..." Libby Gray laughed. "Not that I want to get thrown into a locker again." She pulled out her phone and showed Yani the video of the fires from the High Museum of Art.

"You need my help putting out a fire? "Yani asked confused.

"Yes... and no," I said. "This fire isn't just any object though. It's a person."

"We call him Under King," Janais said.

"A person is causing all this?" Yani said to herself, getting a closer look.

"And we're the only ones who can stop him," I said. "With all of us on the same side, we can capture him and make sure he gets locked up where he should be!" Yani got quiet, continuing to look at the video more.

"This isn't just one fire either," Libby Gray said. "There have been at least four others we know about."

"Have y'all fought him yet?" Yani asked, looking up at us.

"More or less..." Libby Gray whispered.

Yani paused and continue to stare at the video. "The High Museum of Art was my favorite place to go in the summers when my parents were still together. It was one of the few good memories I had with them. It was a rare time when they weren't arguing."

"I didn't know it was that bad with your parents," I said, growing concerned.

"How would you? You left me hanging after I quit the team—you never even asked why I quit." She was right. I was so caught up in my own world I hadn't even paid attention to anyone else's. "Look, I'm in, but I'm not doing this for y'all! I'm doing it because I love that place." We began high-fiving each other and noticed Adeema still standing in the doorway, leaning on the wall.

"FINALLY!" Libby Gray exclaimed. "We can end this!"

"Here's the thing though," Yani said. "If this guy is as bad as y'all say, fighting all cute and stuff isn't going to work. We gotta beat this guy at his own game. Y'all in?"

"We're in!" Libby Gray, Janais and I said.

"Wait, where is the other one?" Yani asked.

"The other one has a name and I'm right here," Adeema said, folding her arms.

"Oh, get over yourself. Are you in or what? You may not like me, but you need me!"

Adeema rolled her eyes and sighed. "Fine, I'm in!"

Under King was about to be in a whole new world of pain. Hopefully, we had all we needed to take him down for good.

Libby Gray

We were finally back on the same page. I was busy sketching a surprise suit idea for Yani. If she was going to fight with us, she needed to do it in style. That crop-top-jogger-pants combo was cool and dandy for robbing a corner store, but this was a whole new ballgame. She needed an upgrade. Even though I preferred vibrant colors and patterns, I was trying my hardest to stay true to her love of black and monochromatic colors.

"All I'm saying is y'all need way more aggression when you fight," Yani said. "Y'all can't save everyone. Some people you may have to, you know..."

"Wait—are you talking about killing someone?" Adeema asked looking at the new uniform I'd made for her. I stayed with a similar blue motif and made a new jacket to match the print of her new blue, grey, white and black hijab. Her black hammer pants were also lined with blue to complete the look.

"Look, goody two shoes, I know you think you are above all of that. I'm simply stating it's going to come to the point where it's either him or you. And I know you don't want it to be you." Yani spun around in Janais' chair as everyone was busy trying on their new suits. This had to be how top designers felt seeing their work come to life.

"She has a point!" Kenzie said, looking in the mirror. "We have to end this. We may not be able to save him." I decided to ditch her old cheerleader-like uniform and gave her a sleek jumpsuit she could use to capitalize on her fluid movements and killer gymnastics skills. The rich purple suit had her looking like royalty and the bright yellow band around her waist popped in just the right way. I also decided to give her ankle rider boots to provide the normally preppy Kenzie with some edge.

"See! Someone has some sense!" Yani said.

"I just don't know if I feel comfortable killing someone," Adeema said, sitting on the floor next to me. "That goes against everything I believe in."

"Well, what does your god say about hitting people so hard, it feels like they got punched in the face by an 18-wheeler? Or throwing basketballs at kids so hard, it dents the locker?" Yani asked with a sideeye. Adeema stood there, shocked for a second. "I am not saying the girl didn't deserve it...bu t hey!"

"Yeah well, you *both* deserved it," Adeema said, rolling her eyes.

"Yeah, whatever," Yani said.

"So how do I look?" Janais asked, walking out of the bathroom she had been holed up in for the past hour. Our mouths dropped to the floor as she stood there with her left hand gently placed on her hip. She stood tall in a bright yellow off-shoulder dress with a black belt and pockets, because I knew she loved those. Since it was almost summer, I canceled the tights. I spray painted some of her Chuck Taylor's black and added a yellow lightning bolt on them to match the one on the hem of her dress. We weren't shocked at how great my suit looked on her, because we all knew

I was killer with a needle and thread. It was her hair. Her usual curls had been straightened and were resting easily down the middle of her back.

"YOUR HAIR!" Adeema exclaimed.

"Does it look okay?" she asked, fidgeting with her uniform.

"YESS!" we yelled in unison. She had so much volume in her hair, it put my big mane to shame.

"Y'all really look good!" Yani said, getting a closer look at Janais' suit. "I'm slick jealous."

"No need to be. I have you covered too!" I said, drawing the finishing touches on her design.

"What do you mean?"

"I'm talking about this! "I said showing her the sketch I had just finished as the girls hurried together to get a better view.

"I don't even know what to say," she said, looking at the design.

"What? Yani is speechless?" Adeema said.

"Oh hush!" Yani joked. "This is just too good."

Janais pointed to the paper. "Is that a trench coat?"

"Yes, it's thin though, so you don't have to worry! I always see you at school with those oversized jackets so I thought I would design you your own. Now underneath is where it gets a little fun. I sketched you a black crop top that has an exaggerated hood that can cover your eyes when you want to be secretive."

"*Muy caliente,*" Kenzie said.

"Oh, and the crop top and distressed jeggings are both lined with grey to match your new trench. You know... that eerie undercover vibe you like so much."

"This is a lot. Will you be able to get this done before we try to find Under King tomorrow?"

"Girl my hands are faster than Janais' speed," I said assuring her. "The Kids Are Alright" began playing out of Janais' Bluetooth speakers at the perfect time and we all instantly began to bop our heads to the melody.

"This is my song!" Yani squealed.

"What do y'all know about Chloe X Halle?" Janais asked. The girls started dancing around the room, hands all in the air. The calm before the storm.

I caught a glimpse of myself in the mirror. I was so focused on everyone else's suit, I hadn't even looked at mine. The military had not been good to my family, so I scrapped the army fatigues, but stayed with the same pink, black, and green hues. The two black triangles on the left and right side on the jumpsuit gave a slimming affect. The new V-neck opened up my chest and gave me room to breathe. It was simple yet chic.

"Everything is new cause we about that innovation
Call it how we see it we a genius generation"

We sang so loud, I was sure the neighbors heard us. Janais was singing into a brush, Kenzie was spinning around like a ballerina, and even Adeema was dancing surprisingly. I took my phone out and recorded the party that was taking place. Everyone seemed truly happy. Time had halted for us and we were awarded a few short moments to just be teenagers. We collapsed as the song came to an end and let out a collective sigh.

"So, how are we going to do it?" Adeema asked, taking off her hijab to fan herself.

"How are we going to do what?" I asked.

"Capture Under King and clear our names."

"Well, I have something up my sleeve for that," Kenzie said, pulling up all her hair in a ponytail. We all sat up, knowing what that look meant.

"What's the plan?" Yani asked, resting her head on her knee.

"One thing we know is that this guy has a fascination with art."

"There is also a lot of buzz on the dark web surrounding the items that were missing," Janais said. "I've been tracking them after we speculated he was stealing art. Many of those pieces are currently being sold. "

"Wait, who just randomly tracks the dark web?" I joked. "Isn't that some secret society, Illuminati stuff?"

"I mean, yeah... kind of. The IP addresses are constantly changing as well as the passcodes—but it's a rather simple algorithm once you learn the pattern," Janais said with a shrug.

"Only you would have a hobby that involves algorithms and illegal activity," Adeema laughed.

"What does any of that have to do with capturing him?" Yani asked.

"Only way to catch a rat is to set a trap," Kenzie said. We looked at each other, still unsure of what she was talking about. "We know this guy has a thing for rare art pieces, right? So we're going to set up a fake art show! We know he'll show up, because he can't resist rare pieces worth millions. We'll catch him in the act, get enough evidence to clear our names and make sure that joker gets locked up!" Kenzie said as we just looked at here. There was about a millisecond of silence before we all started asking questions at the same time.

"A whole art show?" Janais asked.

"How are we supposed to do that?" Adeema fussed.

"That's so extra!" Yani said, rolling her eyes. "Even for y'all!"

"How are we supposed to capture him once he gets there?" I asked confused.

Kenzie just looked at us and smiled before folding her arms. "Don't worry—I got that covered too."

Adeema

Kenzie had come up with some crazy ideas before, but this one was clinically insane. She had explained the plan four times now and I still wasn't getting it. *How were we going to pull this off?* "Okay, maybe one more time," I said, trying to really focus. "What am I doing again?"

"It's not just you! The only way this plan works is if we all work together," Kenzie explained. "Libs, you know how to create buzz on social media. We need you to create an art event that will get everyone talking. Make sure it's a private event though. People love things that they can't get into... take the Met Gala, for example. Really sell it! Make people think we're going to have incredibly rare art pieces. Under King, as predictable as he, will crash anyways."

"I think I can do that. I'll need help bypassing the preset algorithms, so we can make sure he sees the event and everyone else buzzes over it," Libby Gray said, looking at Janais.

"No problem," Janais said, pulling out her laptop. "I can do that!"

"We'll also need to set up surveillance of the building, so we have ears and eyes on him at all times."

"Where is this art show going to be exactly?" I asked, starting to finally understand the plan.

"That's the only part I haven't figured out yet. We need something artsy, yet secluded," Kenzie said, pacing the floor.

"What about the old abandoned paper factory on Chamblee?" Yani asked.

"That could work—the police are just a few blocks away. The parking is inside the garage shared by the building next door, so he probably wouldn't even notice the difference."

"That all sounds all fine and dandy, but what are we supposed to do when we actually get him there?" Yani asked, still not completely convinced of the plan.

"We are all a force separately, but it's going to hard to overpower someone who has zero remorse when it comes to hurting someone," Kenzie said, taking a seat on Janais bean bag. "So that means we are going to have to work together and hit him with everything we got from every angle all at once."

I began to think about Kenzie's plan. It could possibly work. Other than our abilities, our greatest strengths were the fact that we were relying on each other. Working together was the only thing that would bring us home after this whole ordeal.

"So that means we aren't holding back, right?" Yani asked.

"No, not at all!" Kenzie said. "Yani bring the rain, Janais bring the thunder. Adeema punch *through* his face if you have to! Libs, keep him dizzy and we got this!"

We were all pumped now. Janais and Libby Gray began to work on building up the art show.

"Well, I need a sparring partner," Yani said. "It's been awhile since I actually fought. What about you, Adeema?" I felt so indifferent towards her, but if it gave me an opportunity to get one up on her, I was with it.

I stood up to join her in the middle of the room while the other girls busied themselves with Kenzie's plan. I raised my fist to my face, placing one foot slightly forward and beginning to rock front to back. "Are you sure you are ready for a problem like me?" I said, mocking Yani.

"Ha! Try me!" Yani said, throwing her fist in my direction. I ducked and tagged her stomach with the back of my right hand.

"One," I called out with a smile. The last time we went head to head, she got knocked out, so I knew she wasn't going to take it easy on me, but it still felt good to get the first tap in.

"Lucky shot," Yani said, pulling the hair out of her face. "Don't get too happy though—it'll be your last."

"Be nice!" Kenzie yelled from the other side of the room.

"We are!" Yani and I yelled back. She spun around quickly and kicked me right through my ribs.

"One," she said with a grin.

"Okay, time to quit playing!" I said, beginning to roll up my sleeves just as Yani charged towards me. She tried to hit me in the face, but I grabbed her wrist, twisting her arm around and flipping her to the ground, forcing the room to shake. The girls ran toward Yani, trying to help her up.

"I thought we told y'all to play nice!" Kenzie fussed, looking at me.

"Chill. I'm good," Yani said, shaking off the help.

"That's two by the way," I said, holding up two fingers and looking at Yani clench her jaw.

"Can y'all kill each other another day!" Kenzie begged. We need you both to beat Under King!"

"Yeah, chill out!" Janais said, surging electricity in her hands and standing between us.

"We were just playing... right, Adeema?" Yani said, folding her arms.

"Yeah—just playing," I said, leaning back on the wall. "No worries." I rolled my eyes and pulled out my phone. She wasn't worth the hassle. We had a bigger problem to face tomorrow and I didn't need to burn myself out on her.

"Hug it out!" Libby Gray said, looking at Yani and I. We scrunched our faces up in disgust.

"Nah, I'm good on all that," Yani said.

"Me too!

"Nope. Hug!" Kenzie fussed.

Before I could say no, my body began to move towards Yani against my will. It was like I had no control over my body. "What's happening?" I screamed, wondering why my arms were opening. Yani began floating towards me as well.

"I SAID HUG!" Kenzie yelled.

"Wait, are you doing this, Kenz?" Yani squealed as she forcibly embraced me. She smelled of cocoa butter and spearmint gum. The girls began to laugh as Yani and I hovered in the air, hugging against our will.

"Okay, fine! We're hugging! Now put us down!" I said, whining. "This has to be a violation of space!"

Kenzie dropped her hands and we fell onto the ground with a loud thud.

"Dang Kenz, that wasn't even cool!" Yani said, rubbing her head after hitting it against the bed. "Now my head hurts."

"You may not like each other, but you have to learn to respect each other enough to get along," Kenzie said, staring at us.

"Now can we get back to work?" Libby Gray asked, placing her hands on her hips. "Social media buzz isn't created overnight... well, it is *sometimes*. But you know what I mean—we have to get to work."

"Okay fine," I said, standing up. I reached out my hand to Yani. "Truce?"

Yani thought for a second before responding. "Truce," she said, offering her fist in solidarity. It was time to put all our focus on stopping Under King.

Chapter 8

Janais

I carefully unwrapped my hair and stared in the bathroom mirror intensely. I was uneasy—not because I was nervous if my hair had survived my wild sleeping, but because this mission was a lot. I felt like I had been holding my breath since Kenzie told us the plan yesterday. I was hoping and praying we were able to pull this off.

The notifications on my phone had been going crazy all night. It got so bad, I had to put it on silent. People were starting to talk about the Art in the Dark show we made up. Between Libby Gray's social skills and my tech skills, going viral was that much easier. Now we had to wait and see if it would all pay off.

I heard a knock on my bathroom door. There was no point in answering since I knew they would come on in anyway. "Hey, are you decent?" my mom asked, popping her head in.

"Yeah, just doing my hair," I said, refusing to break eye contact from the mirror.

"YOU STRAIGHTENED IT!" she exclaimed. "Awww, my baby! No, you're a little woman. You're so beautiful!"

"I did it yesterday," I said, trying to act unfazed from the elephant in the room. Every time I saw my parents, I began replaying the lies they had fed me over the years. Even still, I wanted to hug her and tell her how proud I was that my hair had grown three inches when I did a length check. But my pride wouldn't let that wall come down.

"I'm sorry, baby. I wish I could have done it with you. It looks great. I have some coconut oil in my bathroom to give it that extra shine if you want," she said, running her fingers through my hair with her manicured nails. "You know I love you right?"

Her words sounded like the sweetest lullaby in that moment—that perfect song that I needed to hear. Words became superfluous. I reached out to grab her by the waist and held on for dear life. I didn't want to let her go. I couldn't even say anything, but the silence was so comforting. It swaddled me and kept me warm like a newborn baby.

But the moment was quick lived, because my father busted in, screaming nonsense. "We need to talk," he said looking at mom, and then at me giving me a quick kiss on the cheek. "Hey baby, your hair looks beautiful."

"Can it wait a little?" my mom asked.

"It actually can't. It looks like we may be moving forward with the plans for the..." he looked at me again, and then, back at my mother. "...you know..."

"You got the funding? Already!" my mom said as her eyes grew huge.

"I guess with all this fire and chaos... and now, those girls... it gave them a reason to expedite the process," he said, pacing the floor. "We need to leave right now—they are calling an emergency meeting."

"Okay, I understand," she said. "I'll see you later, baby," she said, releasing her grasp. I had no idea what they were talking about but it didn't sound good. *Funding for what? Who called a meeting? And what girls?*

"Love you," they said before exiting. I stared at my reflection, confused as to what had just happened. I grabbed my phone and texted the girls.

Janais: So, are y'all ready?

Libby Gray: I'm working on three hours of sleep. It's been hard to rest with all the yelling.

Yani: I'm widdit! Did the Art in the Dark thing work????

Kenzie Sorry Libs :(I can't imagine how hard that is.

Libby Gray: It's whatever. But #ArtInTheDark is trending though. Everyone wants to know how to get in... even some celebs.

Adeema: We're really about to pull this off.

Kenzie: Janais, can we meet at your house around 5?

Janais: No problem!

"Hey!" Libby Gray said, poofing into my bedroom with an overnight bag on her hip.

"Oh my God, Libs! You have to stop doing that—you almost gave me a heart attack!" I said, hunched over the bathroom sink, trying to catch my breath.

"I'm sorry. My house is World War III right now and I can't take it anymore. Mind if I crash here?" she huffed, throwing her bag on the floor and laying across my bed. I peeked out the bathroom door and noticed she was beginning to make herself comfortable.

"Yeah, I guess so," I said, still trying to catch my breath. "But you really should be more careful! My parents were just in here and you could have gotten caught!"

"Yea... but did I?" she said, quickly moving her eyebrows up and down. I rolled my eyes and went back into the bathroom. I was not about to spend my morning trying to make sense of

Libby Gray Dawson. There wasn't enough time in the world for that.

I sat on the bathroom sink and began scrolling through my phone at the event we'd created. Everyone was buzzing about this mystery soirée. I know Keahi saw it, because I created an ad specifically for him and made sure to show it across all his social media accounts. Subliminal messaging at its finest.

I leaned back on my mirror and took a deep breath. The last time I was face-to-face with Under King, I allowed my emotions to get the best of me. If I was going to help defeat him, I had to learn to control my emotions and use them effectively. I breathed in and out slowly, trying to calm myself and get ready for what was to come.

Suddenly, Libby Gray appeared in the bathroom without notice. "LIBBY GRAY!" I yelled, startled once again and looking at all the lightbulbs I had just busted. "Dang, Libs! Will you quit doing that! I've already had to replace these lightbulbs three times this month!"

"I'm sorry," she said, beginning to help me pick up the glass. "I poofed myself into the tub by accident a few days ago and slipped and fell. It wasn't a pretty fall at all," she said, showing me a small scar on her thigh. I shook my head and laughed. Leave it to her to make me laugh right after I had been so mad at her. We sat on the floor of my ill-lit bathroom and laughed while exchanging failed abilities stories. It was nice to know I wasn't the only one who fumbled with my powers.

Kenzie

Eight... nine... ten, I counted off as I stretched in my bedroom. I looked at the clock, the time read 4:00 P.M. It was almost time to meet. I leaned forward and touched my toes as my mind wandered to the mission ahead. Self-doubt crept in like a thief in the night. *Would I be able to lead these girls to victory like I had in the past? Was I a capable leader? Would I be enough?* Even with supernatural abilities, I still battled with inadequacy. I knew I would try my hardest, but what if my best just wasn't enough?

"*Que pasa, Kenzie?*" my brother asked, knocking on my door I forgot to close.

"*No mucho y tu?*" I said, taking a break from stretching and sitting on my floor.

"Doesn't seem like nothing," Carlos said, sitting down next to me. "You have that weight of the world look in your eyes." I hated how in tune he was with me sometimes. *Why couldn't he be a normal oblivious younger brother?* But I came to realize he wasn't normal. Carlos was special—he always had been.

"I'm fine, I promise," I said, kissing the top of his head. "I just have a lot on my mind. Nothing to worry *mi hermano quapo* about."

"Look Kenzie, you gotta breathe sometimes," he said, laying on my lap. "When I'm gone, I need to know you're going to be okay."

"NO! Don't say that! You're going to be here forever. We're going to grow old together and live until we're at least 103." I pulled him closer. I hated when he would talk about not being here. He was going to beat cancer. He was stronger than me and I knew he was going to make it.

"I'm just saying, Kenz! Trust yourself. You're amazing—don't you know that? Quit worrying so much. You're going to end up with wrinkles like abulita!" He laughed and I held him close as warm tears rolled down my cheeks. He was right. I needed to start trusting in myself. He was so wise for such a little man.

"Knock knock!" I looked up to see Adeema and Yani standing in my doorway. "We're not interrupting anything, are we?"

"Nope. I was just bugging my sister. " Carlos hopped out of my lap and turned to give me a smile before walking out my door . *Why was he so perfect?* I thought to myself, wiping my cheek.

"Yo Kenz, you good? " Yani asked, handing me a tissue.

"Yeah, I'm great... *now.*" A huge smile spread across my face, and for the first time in a while, it was authentic. "Let me grab my bag. Y'all ready? Is everything on schedule?"

"Yes indeed. The tech savvy one—" Yani said.

"Janais, you mean..." Adeema cut her off.

"Yeah, *that one*—well, she hacked into his phone thanks to some Wi-Fi near his house. And guess who was searching for directions to our event?"

"And surveillance cameras have been placed around the building," Adeema said, grabbing my bag off the floor. "Thanks to Nay and Libs, we have eyes and ears everywhere."

"Looks like we're right on track then." I pulled my hair into a pony tail and shoved my new suit in my bag before we headed out the door. I kissed my parents on the cheek and hugged my brother. We had all told our parents we were going over to Janais' house to work on a project—we just didn't specify what kind.

"So how are we getting to Nay's house?" I asked, closing the door behind me. "Yani, that was your assignment, right?"

"Our Uber should be pulling up now," Yani said, looking at her phone.

"UBER?" we exclaimed.

"What? Y'all too bougie to ride in an Uber?" Yani said, walking up to a burnt-orange Kia Soul.

Adeema and I looked at each other nervously. "Don't people get killed in Ubers?" she asked, linking her arms in mine.

"Chill, it's just my cousin. It's cool," Yani laughed as she swung open the door. "What's up, cuz!"

"Why didn't you say that!" I exclaimed, hopping in the back seat. Adeema wasn't as sold. She sat so close to me, I could barely put my seatbelt on.

Yani hopped in the passenger's seat and high-fived her cousin before turning to look at us in the back. "Y'all good? " she said, leaning over the passenger's seat before turning to strap on her seat belt. Adeema and I nodded excessively. "I can't believe She-Hulk is scared of an Uber ride."

Adeema rolled her eyes and opened her phone. "Shut up!"

"Everyone in?" her cousin asked, looking in her rearview mirror. She was the spitting image of Yani. Her curly locs were a vibrant red and had all kinds of hair jewels in it.

"Yes ma'am," we said. We began our commute to Janais' house, mumbling along to the music on the radio. The closer we got to her house, the higher my anxiety increased. As much as I was ready to take on Under King, I was still immensely apprehensive despite the talk with my brother. I texted Janais to let her know we were on the way. I began scrolling on my phone through missed texts, unanswered tweets and gossip blogs. Staci had fussed at me via Snapchat about blowing off practice with her again. We were supposed to be coming up with a routine for competition, but my mind had been everywhere but cheerleading. I hadn't done a pike, herkie or toe touch since God knows when. I know Staci was growing tired of my flakiness, but I didn't know how to juggle both lives. It all seemed to be crashing together.

"Kenz, what's up with your friend?" Yani said, breaking my concentration. Yani's cousin began mumbling something in a language very similar to French.

"Why is Libs waving her arms like that?" Adeema said as we pulled into Janais' driveway. Libby Gray ran up to the car and slapped her hands on the window and began screaming something, but the radio was too loud to make it out.

"YaYa you better get your friend! Tell her to get her fingers off my car!" Yani's cousin said, looking over her glasses at Libby Gray who was now trying to open the locked door. "I just cleaned it."

"I got her! No need to hurt anyone!" Yani laughed before getting out. "But thanks Jazz. Oh, and remember—you don't know anything about this."

"Yeah, yeah. Just keep your butt out of trouble," she responded, looking at herself in the mirror and reapplying her lipstick.

"Don't I always!" Yani said, popping her head back in the car.

"Actually, you *don't*," she said, shaking her head. "That's the problem! And watch out for that little redheaded one. She seems crazy."

"She is!" we yelled. Adeema and I gave our thanks and hopped out the car as well, watching Jazz back out the driveway and drive down the street.

"What's all the fuss, Red?" Yani asked, folding her arms.

"GPS shows Under King just pulled open directions to Art in the Dark," Libby Gray exclaimed. "He's on the way!"

"ALREADY?!" we yelled.

"It's only five," I said, checking the clock on my phone. "The flyer says it doesn't start 'til eight!"

"I guess he figured he'd hit the place before anyone got there," Adeema said.

"That's a smart move, actually," Yani said as we all cut our eyes at her. She shruggedl "What? It is."

"Y'all have to hurry up and get ready, so I can get us there before he does. Luckily, he's still an hour away," Libby Gray said, pacing the driveway.

"What are we waiting for?" I said, running inside. "Let's get to it!"

Libby Gray

We all stood in the mirror, squeezed tightly together trying to get one last look of ourselves to see if we were ready. Janais' room was completely trashed. Clothes were everywhere from us rushing to get ready. But through all that chaos, we came together and we looked good.

"I'm not one to toot my own horn, but..." I said, looking in the mirror at all the creations I made.

"Yes, you are. That's literally all you do, Libs," Adeema said, adjusting her hijab.

"ANYWAYS! I am just saying," I said, fluffing my already larger-than-life hair. Yani does everything fit okay? I had to guess your measurements in some areas since you insist on wearing those ugly, oversized clothes. Which is so NOT the move, B-T-dubs. You be looking hobo chic."

" I know you think we're all best friends and what not since we're working together," Yani said, staring at me in the mirror. "But trust, we're not that cool for you to be talking crazy with me like that. You got it?" Sometimes, my mouth got me in trouble and this was one of those times. All I could do was nod and hope her glare wouldn't kill me. "But yes, everything looks and feels great. This coat is so light and the crop top hoodie is fly!"

"Alright, enough of that!" Kenzie said, securing her bun on her head. "He should be there any minute."

"Under King just turned on Jefferson Parkway—that's only fifteen minutes away from the Art District. " Janais said, swiping on her phone.

"What are we waiting for then? " Kenzie said as we all held hands.

"Everyone ready?" I said.

"Ready!" they all said in unison. I took a deep breath and jumped us to the back of the abandoned paper factory. Thankfully, nothing was there but stray cats and a ton of trash.

"What in the world is that smell!" Kenzie asked, covering her face.

"I think it's coming from the dumpster," Yani said.

"Let's hurry up and get inside before the smell attaches itself to us," Kenzie said still covering her nose.

"Who has the key?" Janais' asked.

I pulled out my old Cash App card and a bobby pin from my hair. "Well, it's not a key, but I know how to get in." After a few shimmies and some brute force, we were in. *The things you learn on YouTube.* We walked into the empty warehouse, which still smelled of fresh paper.

"Alright, it's time to get set up," Kenzie said, closing the door behind us. "How much time until he gets here?"

"About ten minutes... maybe sooner, depending on traffic on Main Street," Janais said, looking at her phone.

"Okay bet! Nay, Yani... y'all make sure the surveillance from the surrounding building is set up and put it..." Kenzie paused looking over the warehouse for the ideal place to put the laptop that would be recording everything before finally pointing. "Over there by those crates, on top of the boxes. Then y'all can get ready to guard the back door." Yani and Nay nodded their heads before running off to complete their tasks and guard their post. "Adeema, hit the lights and turn the speaker on, so we can create the illusion of someone being here."

"Someone *is* here," I said, confused.

"Someone other than us, silly!" Kenzie said, shaking her head. Adeema grabbed the speaker and ran off into the warehouse.

"What about me? " I asked, eager for my assignment.

"You're going to stay right here in the middle. Just in case he gets past any of us, you have to be here to slow him down," Kenzie said, placing her hand on my shoulder.

"Where will you be?" I asked.

"I'll be guarding the front doors. Don't worry, Libs—all our Bluetooth devices are connected, so we're only a holler away. "

She began running towards the front of the building while I stood there in the middle of the warehouse. I found myself twirling my curls like Janais did when she was nervous. I took out my phone, hoping a comfort selfie would ease my tension. "Ugh, the lighting in here is terrible," I said aloud, beginning to walk around, trying to find the best light for a picture.

"R.E.S., come in. Anyone have eyes on Under King yet?" Kenzie asked. I had to turn the volume down a bit, because she was killing my eardrums.

"I'm not part of R.E.S!" Yani snapped. "This is a one-time thing!"

"We know that!" Janais laughed. I held my phone up at a 90-degree angle where I usually took my best photos.

"All good over here too!" Adeema answered.

"Well he hasn't reached y'all, so you know he hasn't made it to me," I said, continuing to try and find the best angle. *There we go... almost perfect.* I waited for my phone to focus. "Okay Google... take a picture!" I said as my phone began counting down.

Three...

Two...

Suddenly, there was a huge crash overhead. I covered my head to shield myself from the glass as the crash forced me to the ground.

"What was that noise?" Adeema yelled.

"Is everyone okay?" Kenzie said.

My head was pounding from a wood panel that had fallen on top of me. I shook off the glass and debris that had fallen all around me.

I rose to see Under King staring at me with a smile. "Hello Red!"

"Y'all, he's here!" I yelled quickly, dusting myself off and getting ready to give him a top-tier butt whooping. He started manipulating fire in his hands.

"Not this time!" I yelled, poofing away from his glare. I teleported myself onto his back and began punching him as hard as I could on his head. My legs held on as I hit him with everything I had.

" You're even more annoying than the little one!" he said, trying to shake me off. "And don't you know you're heavy? Get off me!"

"Don't you know you're a criminal? You don't get to have a say!" I said, squeezing my legs tighter. He grabbed ahold of my arm and threw me over his shoulder into a pillar.

"It's over, Red! Now stay out my way, I have art to collect and a legacy to continue! Now, where is it?" Under King growled, making fireballs in each of his hands. I laid on the ground, struggling to get up and trying to conceal my obvious pain. Everything was hurting, but there was no way I could show him that. "I SAID, WHERE IS THE ART!" He threw a fireball at the pillar I was leaning against. Before I could even catch my breath, he cocked his hand back and slapped me clear across my face, forcing me to stop breathing for a second. My lips quivered as I tried to speak. I choked on the blood swarming in my mouth and looked at Under King with so much rage. This tasted like the end.

Adeema

I leapt over the banister from the second floor exit I was guarding. When I landed, I hit the ground harder than expected and crushed the floor beneath me. Libby Gray's screams still echoed in my ears. I ran to her as quickly as I could with my hijab blowing in the wind behind me. "Hold on, Libs! I'm on the way!" I leaped over stacks of debris, stacks of wood, abandoned furniture and fixtures.

"Hurry," Libs whimpered.

"Just teleport out of there, girl!" Yani said. "We'll handle him!" I knew I was almost to Libby Gray, but all I heard was Under King's obnoxious voice.

"I can't... I'm too—" Libby Gray's voice faded out. I turned the corner where she was supposed to be and halted in my place.

"Take another step and we're going to see how quickly Lil' Red Not From The Hood burns!" Under King snarled with one arm wrapped around Libby Gray's neck. She was crying and her normal emerald eyes were now a deep blue. I didn't know what to do. Everything I could think of would only put her in more danger. I looked to my left and saw Janais and Yani, with Kenzie to my right. We formed a circle around Under King and Libby Gray. "You know... I'm starting to think this was a set up!"

"Guess you're not as stupid as you look," Kenzie said, raising her fists and preparing to fight.

"Give it up, Under King! We have you surrounded," Janais said, revving up her electrical abilities.

"I see Georgia Power is back on. You didn't get enough last time?" Under King said, turning in the circle to get a better look at all of us before dragging Libby by the neck with him.

"Cut the crap and let our friend go, you pyromaniac brute!" I yelled, stomping my foot on the ground and causing the building to shake. The girls cut their eyes at me, trying to brace themselves.

"Wait... one, two, three, four... *five*? Did the pint-sized heroes recruit someone else to get their butt kicked too?" Under King laughed. Yani shrugged and looked up through the broken ceiling. There was a storm brewing. Thunder started to boom so loudly, it made it hard to hear. His eyes bounced from Yani to the ruckus above. He smirked and nodded, almost in approval before going back to his menacing stare. He was halted by a wood panel crashing down by his feet. "Did you just—?" He threw Libby Gray against the wall and launched fiery darts in our direction. "Is this about all those paintings I borrowed?"

I quickly ran to Libby Gray's aid who was gasping for air. I hated seeing her like this. Janais began throwing lightning bolts at Under King and the girls started hitting him from every angle.

I had just enough time to check on Libby Gray. "Breathe Libs, I'm here!"

I propped her up against the wall and she grabbed my hand.

"I'm... okay. Go... go end this!" The look in her eyes was one of urgency, so I knew I had to go help. I stood up took a deep breath and leapt towards Under King, landing right behind him with a thud louder than the thunder roaring outside. He turned and I launched him forty feet across the room with a swift right hook. Before he could gain his composure, Kenzie lifted him high in the air and flung her hands around her head, spinning him around in the air like a top.

"My turn!" Yani yelled, lurching towards him. She inhaled a massive amount of air, causing a large tornado to appear which caught Under King in the cross fire. Janais tagged herself in and started throwing lightning bolts inside the tornado as he screamed in agony. It wouldn't be long before he was a distant memory. We were actually doing it—we were going to defeat him.

"Uhm, what's that red thing in the middle?" Janais asked, taking a break from target practice.

We walked closer to the tornado that was already shaking the building. Kenzie grabbed my hand. "It's growing!" The red ball began swelling like a balloon. Yani was hunched over, struggling to keep everything compacted together. Her honey-hued complexion was beginning to turn darker from the pressure of the wind she was producing.

"I don't think she can hold it much longer," Libby Gray said, holding her side as she stood up.

"Do you have the strength to jump us out if it gets too crazy?" Kenzie asked.

Libby Gray rested her body against the pillar. "I think so."

"Well, we're about to find out what's up real soon" I said.

Yani collapsed on the ground as Kenzie ran to grab her. "Remind me... to never... try... that... again," she said, gasping for air. The tornado dissipated in front of us and a huge fire appeared in its place.

"Is he—" I started.

"I don't believe so," Janais said, taking a step back. "He seems to be in some sort of stasis." We could see him hovering in the middle of the fire with his eyes closed.

"Stasis?" Libby Gray repeated, attempting to stand up all the way. "Y'all have to quit making up words..."

"Don't you ever pay attention in Mrs. Jones class?" Janais snapped.

"Even I know that one," Yani said, backing up.

"Homeostasis, Libs!" I interjected.

"Oh, you mean—"

"Not now!" Kenzie said, thankfully silencing the group.

"I think we need to start backing up," Janais said, taking a step backwards.

"Don't you think we need to dispose of this... *whatever it is?*" Kenzie said, waving her arms.

"It took all the energy I had to keep it contained," Yani said, inching backwards another step.

"Maybe I can use my powers to enclose it," Kenzie said, raising her hands.

"That doesn't seem like greatest idea" I said, joining everyone further away from the flame.

"Come on y'all, we can take him!" Libby Gray said, walking closer with Kenzie.

"Uh, you're on your own," Yani snapped. "You already got your butt handed to you once. I'm not keen on getting my tail fried."

"Here goes nothing!" Kenzie said. She raised her long slender arms and extended them forward, giving me Hermione vibes.

She was going to cast a spell on him and I hoped it ended better than before. But just in case it didn't, I remained at a safe distance as the warehouse continued to get hotter. Sweat rolled from under my hijab and I wiped my forehead, trying to gasp for the little air remained. Kenzie began to move the fire while Libby Gray watched nearby. The more Kenzie tried to control the fire, the wilder the flame became.

"I'm trying," Kenzie said struggling. "But I don't think I can—"

"Get out of there!" I yelled. Kenzie and Libby Gray quickly pivoted around and ran in our direction. Libby Gray grabbed Kenzie's arm and jumped them towards us. Under King emerged from the flames like a phoenix, levitating with his arms stretched out and his long wavy mane intertwined with the fire surrounding him. The name Under King had become very befitting. He looked like something that had crawled from the depths of the underworld.

"This isn't even close to being over, is it?" I asked as we all gathered closely together.

"Not even in the slightest" he said, beginning to move towards us.

Chapter 9

Janais

This guy will not quit! I thought to myself. We had all tried to take him on and nothing was working. The oxygen in the air was thinning and the humidity was awful, so I was certain that my hair looked like a giant cotton ball. But we had bigger issues than my wild hair. *How were we going to stop someone who was unstoppable?* "Kenz, what are we going to do?" I whispered.

"He's too stong!" Libby Gray said.

"Giving up isn't an option—we have to fight until we can contain him and then call the police," Kenzie said, securing her hair tighter.

"If *we* can't contain him, how are the police supposed to?" Yani snapped.

"We'll have to worry about that later. Now we have to fight!" Kenzie said, running towards him. We all followed suit, screaming out our loudest war cries as he began launching fireballs. We countered everything he threw at us.

"Nay, duck!" Adeema yelled, throwing everything she could get her hands on at Under King. I looked to my left and saw a fire ball speeding towards me. I tucked and rolled into a somersault, launching a lightning bolt towards him as I rolled up.

"Kenz, get me close!" Adeema said. "I have an idea."

"Cover us!" Kenzie instructed. I sped around Under King and tried to distract him as Libby Gray jumped around him. Every time she reappeared, she would strike him with a wood panel she had picked up from the floor. Yani joined in and created wind and rain. Kenzie levitated Adeema in the air, bringing her right to him. I hadn't exerted this much energy in my entire life. I was running as fast as my feet would allow.

"Almost there," Adeema said in our Bluetooth. "Keep him centered."

"I'm trying!" Libby Gray yelled, hitting him in his side and jumping away before he could retaliate.

The vein in the middle of his head pulsated. He didn't know what to react to, and every time he tried to generate fire from him hands, Yani would wash him out. "Not this time!" she laughed, showering down a heavy rain. The vein in the middle of his head looked like it was going to explode.

"Psst! Hey!" Adeema said, tapping his shoulder from behind. Under King turned around quickly only to be met by her fist to the face, knocking him to the ground instantly and forcing the floor to cave in around him. Unable to move, he groaned in defeat. We circled around him as he lay in a fetal position.

"Now it's time to finish the job," Yani said, cracking her knuckles. "We gotta kill him."

"Wait, are we were serious about... *killing* him?" I whispered.

"Yes, we have to!" Yani said, looking for one of us to back her up.

"Isn't it enough that I broke his nose and probably his jaw?" Adeema said. "He can't even stand, and even if he could, Nay spun him so dizzy, he can't even tell up from down."

"I can't believe y'all are punking out on me right now! Bailing on the plan. Don't y'all remember everything he did! He's the bad guy!"

"You were the bad guy a few months ago, and we didn't kill *you!*" Adeema barked back as he laid unconscious, barely breathing.

"The police should be here shortly," I said, looking at my phone and heading to the computer as quickly as I could to finalize the recording of us fighting Under King.

"Oh, I know you didn't just compare me to *him!*"

"Y'all are both criminals by most standards. We showed you mercy—why not him?" Adeema asked. Just when I thought the heat was subsiding, it began to heat up in a whole new way.

Yani tied her locs back as if she was preparing for another round. "Last time I checked, being a masked vigilante with a God complex is against the law too!"

"We can argue about who is right and wrong all day, but we have to do something before he wakes up," Kenzie said, trying to be the mediator. I copied the video file to a jump drive and fastened it to a chain before placing it around Under King's neck and attaching a note with WATCH ME written across it.

"Man, forget y'all. I'm out!" Yani pulled her hood over her head and turned for a quick exit. "Since I'm *just like* Under King, I don't want to tarnish anyone's good girl image." Her grey trench coat whipped around behind her swiftly, dancing in the wind.

"Come on Yani, don't go!" Kenz pleaded.

She turned back around slowly. "No. I don't want to be the bad girl you only want to use when you need someone to help you from getting your tails handed to you," she said before disappearing into the shadows.

Kenzie

"Try her phone again," I pleaded as the girls paced the floor.

"We'll have to worry about Yani later," Janais said, grabbing my hand as I looked in her eyes and took a deep breath. "The police should be around the corner by now."

"Okay, Libs, Nay... y'all grab the equipment," I instructed trying to refocus. "Adeema and I are taking Under King to the front and handing him over to the police."

"Gotcha, here is the video," Nay said handing me the USB and a note.

"Hurry!" I said, shooing them off as Janais grabbed Libby Gray's hand before she had a chance to question my directions.

"I can't believe that brat just left us like that. How could—"

"Save it, Adeema!" I said, cutting her off. "Grab Under King. I'll get the doors." He was about two hundred pounds, and even unconscious, he still looked like he could do damage. Adeema huffed and bent over to grab him, tossing him over her shoulder with ease.

Janais' voice echoed in my ear from my Bluetooth. "People are beginning to migrate outside! Be careful."

"Probably here for the art show. Too bad the only piece of work we have is hanging over my shoulder," Adeema laughed. I rolled my eyes and pushed open the double doors to see at least a hundred people waiting to get inside.

"Uhm, guys it's way more than a few people," I said into my Bluetooth.

"OH MY GOD! It's Dynamic & Moxie!" a woman exclaimed.

"Those are the hooligans responsible for the fire at the High

Museum of Art!" yelled a man resembling Uncle Ruckus. Being face-to-face with the type of people who were saying those hurtful things online was not fun at all. It was time to set the record straight. I looked out to see the news and police arriving.

"Yes, the Royal Elite Squad was at the scene of that terrible fire," I said, stepping forward using my cheer voice to command the crowd.

"See, I knew those girls were trouble!" the man yelled again. "The police are the only ones that need to be handling criminals!" There were others in the crowd who screamed out in agreeance.

"Yeah, because the police do such a good job with that," a kid shouted sarcastically while holding his phone up to the man's face to record him. "How many people have they gunned down for no reason at all?"

I looked at Adeema in the doorway and nodded for her to come out. "The real criminal behind the fires, going all the way back to the one on the 85 bridge is Under King!" I pointed to Adeema and the crowd erupted in chatter.

"And it's all on this drive!" she said, waving the USB in the air. The crowd started yelling and the police officers had to intervene to contain the crowd. "I think we need to get out of here, Kenz..."

"I agree. Libs, we need a hand," I said into the Bluetooth, backing up as reporters began to close in.

A Fox 5 News representative called out from behind the barriers the police had put up. "Dynamic, how many other government-tested failed experiments like you are there?"

"How does it feel to be Atlanta's hero again after such awful allegations?" A Channel 2 reporter asked, pushing in front of the reporter from Fox 5.

"We're on the way!" Libby Gray said.

"Hurry, it's getting hectic out here!"

"Freeze! You're under arrest. Get your hands up!" An officer yelled out. A dozen officers surrounded us, pointing guns at two girls who were just trying to help. Unfortunately, our reward wasn't a key to the city, but a Glock 22.

"Y'all gonna shoot them for helping?" an older lady yelled out. An officer moved quickly to restrain her and madness exploded. Half the crowd was pro-Royal Elite Squad and the rest thought we were circus freaks. Officers continued to point their weapons in our direction and my heart dropped to the soles of my feet. I instantly began praying and crying. I was petrified and paralyzed with fear as my heart began to beat out of my chest. Having an officer point a gun at me was almost expected as a person of color, but it didn't make the experience any easier to handle. I didn't want to be another Latina gunned down by the hands of the police.

"Libs, where are y'all?"

"Put your hands on your head!" the officer yelled again. I could see the officer's finger on the trigger, ready to shoot.

Adeema and I let go of each other's hands and started to raise them in the air slowly, trying not to make any sudden moves. "Kenzie, do something," Adeema's voice cracked as she fought back tears.

I refused to go out like this. I flicked my hands in the air quickly and the officers' guns did the same, dangling in the air as the roaring crowd instantly became silent.

"This is the thanks we get for trying to save this city?" Adeema yelled with tears rolling down her cheeks. "We didn't ask for this!"

Finally, Janais and Libby Gray appeared. "Sorry we're late," Libby Gray said, grabbing my arm. She turned around to see the crowd and the weapons in the air. In an instant, she poofed us away and we landed in Janais' room where Adeema and I started to break down. We were trying to save a city that obviously didn't want to be saved.

Libby Gray

I spun around in Janais' desk chair, staring at the ceiling. It had been hours since the debacle and my lower half was still aching from Under King tossing me around like a Raggedy Ann doll. Normally after a win, we would be celebrating with tons of music and lots of good food, but this victory sucked.

Kenzie sighed and began to pace the floor. "She's still not answering her phone." She had been calling Yani non-stop since we got back to Janais' house. "She was finally coming around and we just had to go and ruin it."

"Well, it was really because of Adeema, to be honest," I said, still spinning.

"LIBS!" Janais yelled out.

"What? It's the truth—Adeema has been giving her a hard time ever since she joined us. She's the one who pushed her away!"

"Don't pin this all on me!" Adeema fussed. "You want to talk about blame? What about you, Libby Gray! What took you so long to come get us? Your only useful ability is that you can teleport and you couldn't even do that."

"Hey, cut it out!" Janais yelled, standing with half of her hair two-strand twisted and the other half still wet and curly from the shower. "We're not the enemy here. Fighting amongst ourselves isn't going to solve anything!" We all looked at her shocked. "Look, I know that's saying a lot coming from me, but you should take my word that much more."

"Do you see what they are saying about us though?" Adeema asked with her face in her phone. "Like, come on—this idiot posted on the Fox 5 page that he 'doesn't feel safe with a terrorist running wild.' All we've ever done is save people's lives. But they don't see that—all they see is *this*!" she yelled, yanking off her hijab and beginning to cry.

"Don't let those people get to you!" Kenzie said, handing it back. "We can't let the naysayers shake us."

"Fox 5 News is trash by news standards anyway," Janais said, turning on her TV. "Check this out though."

"Do we have to? "Adeema said covering her face with her hijab.

"I promise you'll want to hear this one," Janais said, turning up the volume on 11 Alive News. "My mom sent me a text about it." We all tuned into the video, even Adeema who was partially covering her ears.

"This is Paul Jones with 11 Alive News, here to give you an update on a story we've been following for the past few months. Early this afternoon, the Royal Elite Squad apprehended the supposed arsonist behind a string of Atlanta fires and art robberies."

"I swear as soon as I hear something crazy, I am punching a hole through your TV," Adeema said.

"Oh hush," Janais said, turning up the volume. "Social media has actually been raving over Channel 11's approach to our story."

"I am utterly amazed—since when do you know so much about social media?" I asked with a laugh.

"Just pay attention!" Janais said with her finger over her lips.

"The Atlanta Police Department has apprehended the person responsible for the fires that have been terrorizing the Metro

Atlanta area. And it's all thanks to the brave efforts of the Royal Elite Squad, and a confession from the person they call Under King," Paul Jones said, flashing his perfect smile.

"Did Paul Jones just call us brave?" Kenzie asked, geeking out.

"You know, I still think it's very awkward that he's your celebrity crush," I said to Kenzie, who was mere inches from the screen, admiring his 80-watt smile.

"My mom says the first crushes are supposed to be weird," Janais said, rolling her eyes. "Mine was Justin Gray in fifth grade."

"Oh, details! Please tell me more!" I squealed.

"Wait... Justin Gray who used to run down the halls with his arms straight back like an anime character?" Adeema joked as the girls began to laugh.

"*Used to?*" Kenzie chimed in. "He went as One-Punch Man for career day a few months ago!"

"Don't judge me," Janais said as her cheeks began to turn red. "He was in all my gifted classes, and he was really sweet... well, before puberty hit."

"Now he's has a mustache, he's grown more than a foot and pull girls' bra straps anytime he gets a chance," Kenzie said, finally taking a step back from the TV.

"Boys," we all said with a laugh.

"Well, I don't think *my* boyfriend is like that," I said.

"Boyfriend?" the girls repeated in unison.

"Yes, my future husband," I said, pulling up a picture of Keahi up from Instagram that had him resembling the Greek god Hercules. I looked up from my phone to see the girls looking at me like I had lost my mind.

"You're clearly delusional," Kenzie said. "All that smoke has gone to your brain."

"He just tried to kill you not even a day ago!" Janais said, shaking my shoulders.

"That was Under King versus Bombshell—not Keahi and Libby Gray," I said with a smile. "Maybe I can help make him better." I was only kidding, but it was funny seeing them squirm with anger and disappointment. I closed my eyes and went back to spinning in the chair. We were breathing a little easier at last. Now, it was time to rest until the next problem appeared.

Adeema

I laid on the floor, trying to sleep, but finding it as easy as a half-court shot. Janais was fast asleep in her bed. Libby Gray had finally fallen asleep after a very heated debate as to why classroom desks were a social construct to confine creativity. Meanwhile, Kenzie laid on the couch and worked on her computer. Channel 11 News played softly in the room, but loud enough that I could hum along to every commercial that came on.

I thought about the crazy events of the day. Most of it was a combination of random circumstances that I had no control over, but there was thing I could change: the way I handled Yani coming into the group was out of line and I needed to apologize. I judged her so harshly. And in the same breath, I was asking the world not to judge me. It wasn't right.

"You're still up?" Kenzie whispered. I looked up from my sleeping bag to see her bright smile illuminating in the dimly lit room.

"I can't sleep, I guess," I said, rolling over to my back. "What's your excuse?"

"Summer camp program applications. Next year, we will

be in ninth grade and I have to start focusing on these college applications if I want to get into a good school when I graduate," she said, typing away on her computer.

"You're thinking about college already? I can barely figure out what I want to eat tomorrow, let alone what I want to do in the next four years. Having to think that far ahead makes my stomach queasy."

"Aren't you going to go to Georgia Tech like your dad?" Kenzie asked, closing her laptop.

"I don't think I have a future in science. That's you and Nay," I whispered.

Kenzie giggled before leaning back to look at the TV. "Hey, what's going on?" Kenzie said, getting up from the couch and beginning to pay attention to whatever was on the screen.

"Who knows? It's late, so they are probably covering all the weird stories no one really cares about right now."

"Uh, no! You're going to want to get up for this one. They are talking about us and Under King." She waved for me to join her as she looked for the remote, throwing clothes, tossing pillows, and tearing the room apart in search of it. I got up and realize I had been laying on it the entire time. "Thanks,"
she said, snatching it before I could give it to her and turning up the volume as loud as it could go. "Janais, Libs... wake up!"

"You better have a really good reason for waking me up from a dream about my future in fashion industry!" Libby Gray said, stretching her arms.

"I second that," Janais said, throwing the cover over her head. "Can't we have just one night where we sleep like regular humans?"

"This is important, listen!" Kenzie said with her eyes glued to the TV.

The girls came and sat on the floor begrudgingly and tried to see what had Kenzie all worked up.

"Police are unsure how this could have happened, but the suspect known as Under King has vanished inside the holding cells at the Atlanta Metro police station around 10 p.m. this evening. There was a disruption that caused some sort of earthquake, and in turn, caused the power to go out, leading to his escape."

"You have to be freaking kidding me!" I said, fighting the urge to punch a hole in the wall.

"So, we did all that for nothing?" Libs Gray, said throwing her hands in the air.

"We're still hopeful that we'll catch Under King again soon," the Atlanta Police Chief said, speaking at the press conference. "The city of Atlanta wouldn't even know who was causing these fires if it hadn't been for the Royal Elite Squad—whoever you are, I thank you and Atlanta thanks you."

I was infuriated. "So, we do our job, catch the jerk and the cops end up losing him? Maybe Yani was right—we should have just killed him. We did everything right and it still feels like we lost."

"No, we were right not to kill him," Kenzie said, rubbing her temples. "We're not murderers."

"That's bogus!" Libby Gray let out. "We wouldn't even be in the wrong for killing someone who caused so much pain and destruction to so many people."

"Hey, we're the good guys—and there's no coming back from something like that." Normally, Kenzie's talks would work on us, but we were too far gone at the moment. It felt like our best just wasn't enough this time.

Chapter 10

Janais

"Janais, Janais! Did you hear what we said?" my dad asked, tapping the table.

I didn't know where my mind was at that moment, but I was not listening. "I'm sorry, I wasn't paying attention. What did you say? " I asked, mixing grits, eggs, and shrimp around on my plate.

He put his hand over mine softly and I was forced to look up. "I said we officially got the backing, so I will officially be running for Governor of Georgia this fall!" He was smiling so hard, I saw all four of his dimples, a feature I once thought I got from him.

"I thought you were already running? Wasn't that what those parties were about?" I asked, somewhat unimpressed. I was still mentally tired from the night before.

"Well, technically yes," mom cut in. "We had to get more endorsements—"

"*Money*," I mumbled.

She cut her eyes at me before finishing. "Well, yes... that too."

"This has been my dream since I was a child," he said, giving her a kiss. "I'm so glad I can finally share that dream with my two favorite ladies!"

"Well congrats," I said, trying to be engaged. "I know this means a lot for you."

"That means the world coming from you," he said, holding my hand tighter. "I am going to need your incredible mind on my campaign too" That idea made me smile a bit. We used to joke that I'd be his chief analyst whenever he ran for a government position, since I knew how things worked and I always knew how to get results. Little did he know, I had been putting that theory to the test over the past few months.

"So, what won the benefactors over in the end? Was it your charming smile?" I asked with a laugh.

"He does have a beautiful smile, huh?" mom said, staring at him and grinning from ear to ear. If it wasn't so gross, it would have been cute.

"Oh, stop it. The platform that I'm running on proposes a lot of new plans and laws that would really help the state, and, in turn, the world."

"Like what?" I asked, slightly intrigued.

"I can't say much yet, baby girl. But it's going to help keep you a lot safer from what's going on in the world, especially here in Atlanta."

"So, you're trying to be super hero now?" I asked with a smile.

He laughed. "Superheroes are only good for TV and movies, dear. The real heroes are firefighters, scientists, teachers, government officials and people of that caliber. Those are the people who make real change." He took a sip of his coffee and I couldn't help but to think on what he'd just said.

"Okay, enough of that," mom said, putting her fork down. "I'm just glad you're talking to us again!"

I laughed. "I couldn't let you all suffer too long."

"Now, more than ever, we need to rely on each other. These next few months will be rigorous, but nothing can stop us when we have each other's backs!" he said, showing off that million-dollar smile.

I went back to eating brunch and allowed my thoughts to carry me off. I didn't have everything figured out and I wan't sure what the future would hold in regards to my family, my emotions or Royal Elite Squad, but I was starting to realize what really mattered was who was standing behind me rather than whatever obstacle was standing in front of me. And that was a powerful thing.

Kenzie

My house rocked from the constant dancing and loud music. It was a fiesta fit for an emperor. Roja vieja & tamales filled my nose with the sweetest of smells. I heard the uproar of laughter and yelling. Someone must have lost in a game of dominos because tio was yelling out *"Tramposo!"* While there was definitely fun to be had downstairs, I was in my room, writing essays and completing applications for summer programs that would help propel me in life after high school. The past few weeks had sent my world into a crazy, uncontrollable roller-coaster that made me nauseous simply thinking about it. I needed something in my life I could control and preparing for my future seemed to be the last thing I had control over. I knew it would cost me some things like celebrating my cousin's twelfth birthday, but I hoped it would be worth it in the end.

Suddenly, there was a loud banging against my door. *"Abrir, Alejandra!* I know you're in there!" someone yelled from the other side of my door. This was the fourth family member that had tried to get me downstairs, but I wasn't budging.

"*Estoy trabajando!*" I said without bothering to see who it was and continuing to work at my computer.

"Open up! It's your abuelita and I don't have time for locked doors!" she said, banging on the door once again. *Aw man, they sent the big guns this time.* They knew I couldn't say no to her. I got up from my desk and made it to my door after dragging my feet.

"*Hola, Abuelita Rose,*" I said, forcing a smile. She cut her eyes at me before pushing the door open and scanning the room for a seat. I followed and awaited the lecture that was coming. She sat on the bed and patted the seat.

"*Siéntate nieta,*" Abuelita Rose said, smelling of sugary treats. A kiss on my forehead led to the first question. "So, why is my beautiful granddaughter stuck up here in this room alone while a whole party goes on downstairs for your cousin?"

I looked at her unsure of how to answer without worrying that a chancla would get thrown in my direction. "It's not that I don't want to be down there—I just have so much work to do. I can't get distracted," I said, unable to make eye contact while fiddling with the drawstrings on my UCLA hoodie.

"What's more important than *familia?*"

"What are you talking about? Mi famila is all I ever think about! Who do you think I'm doing all this for?" I yelled, pulling my hood over my head.

"I'm going to excuse that little outburst, because you seem to be putting yourself under a lot of pressure," she said, pulling my hood off my head and the hair out of my face. "Tell me what is going on."

"I am captain of my cheerleading team... I'm in band... trying to maintain my 4.0 while juggling new friends and old ones. And

I want to get into a good college, so Mama and Papa don't have to worry about me. Not to mention being super—" I caught myself and looked at Abuelita who was fully engaged. "...*super tired.* I'm just tired..." I said, hoping she didn't notice my slip up.

"Well, dear that is certainly a lot. I see a lot of you in me, you know... When I was a little older than you, my parents passed away in a car crash. I was the oldest of four, and instead of allowing my siblings to be split up, I took over as guardian. No eighteen-year-old should have all the responsibilities that I had so early. I was barely keeping myself together." I had always heard stories about Abuelita Rose and how she was everyone's *madre.* She had always been so strong, but I never knew how it all started. "I gave up my dreams to focus on my siblings. We were the first generation here from the Dominican Republic. Pleasing other people was a trait I picked up early, and it was horrible for my sanity," she said, rubbing my back. "I felt like I had to make my parents proud and carry on their dreams for me and my siblings. I allowed that pressure to be something that consumed me. I've worked more days in my life than numbers I can count."

"But you're hard working! What's wrong with that?"

"*Si nieta*, but I didn't live! I didn't have that revelation until my old age and I don't want that kind of life for you. I don't regret the roads I've paved for our family, but I do regret it being at my expense. It's time to live, *hermosa.* You can't live for everyone else. Do what makes Alejandra McKenzie happy, and for Christ's sake—breathe!"

I moved to lay in her lap. "But what about school... and my brother... and everything else?"

"I still want you to try your best, but don't forget to make time for you. That'ss what I forgot along the way. Being a people-pleaser gets you nowhere."

I laughed. "Carlos told me something like that a few days ago."

"Well, *mi nietos* are smart like me, so I expect nothing less. You're too young to have gray hairs like me!" She gave me a tight hug and a big smile. "Now let's go have some fun...what do you say?"

I looked at her warm smile and rich, melanin-infused skin and gave her a deep sigh. "Okay, you're right. Maybe I need a little more fun in my life." I hopped up and reached out my hand to help her up. With my arm linked in hers, we walked out my bedroom door and down to the festivities.

"Kenzie!" everyone yelled as they saw me coming down the stairs and greeted me with so many kisses and hugs.

"I'm glad you joined us, *hija*," Mom said, kissing both of my cheeks. "Your cousins are outside—go and enjoy yourself. You've earned it." I nodded and made a dash outside. My family was right. It was time to start living instead of existing.

Adeema

I laid on the grass with my eyes bouncing up and down with the ball as I tossed it in the air. Mentally, I was all over the place and just needed a few moments to breathe.

"Haven't seen much of you around here..." I heard from behind me. I looked up to see my twin sisters, Amara and Amani. Their midnight-black hair blew gracefully in the wind as they came closer.

"I've been so busy with school, my friends and stuff," I said, continuing to toss the ball in the air.

Amani caught it and laid down next to me as Amara followed, both linking their arms in mine. "So, we talked to Ameen... what's going on with you lately?" Amara asked, nudging my shoulder.

"What do you mean? I'm perfectly fine. School's great, home is great... life is great!"

"That's a lot of greats," Amara said, skeptical of my enthusiasm. "Try again!" they said in unison.

"You may not be our twin, but we can still tell when you're lying. Call it sister-telepathy," Amani said, putting her head on my shoulder.

I sighed. "Okay, I have a question: how do y'all deal with the world constantly judging you based on how you look or your religion?"

"Well, I can tell you it's not easy," Amani said, putting her head on my shoulder as well.

"Staying centered is a must!" Amara said. "Prayer, plus knowing who you are and what makes you happy, goes a long way."

I sighed again. "I have no idea what makes me happy."

"That's not true," Amani answered. "We see the way you light up when a basketball game comes on or when you land a new move you've been working on. "

"But I can't do that with my life," I huffed. "Papa would kill me. You know sports are not a part of his plan for us. If it's not in the trifecta, he doesn't care. Ameen is already working on becoming a doctor, you both got early acceptance into law school, and you know he wants me to be a scientist just like him."

"Therein lies the problem—you're worried about what Papa wants and not what you want!" Amara said, sitting up and noticing the grey streak in her hair she got from our *jida*. She smiled, and for a second, its brightness seemed to eclipse the sun.

"Plus, you suck at science!" Amani said, sitting up to pull her hair up into a bun atop her head.

"Amani!" Amara said, slapping her arm.

"It's true," Amani and I said in unison. They pulled me up from the grass and we laughed together.

"But honestly, Papa will live! If basketball is your happy like proving people wrong is mine, you owe it to yourself to pursue it," Amani said, sitting crisscrossed on the grass.

"At least try out for the team or something," Amara said, scrolling on her phone.

"Well, Coach Smith did ask me if I wanted to try out for the summer league team," I said bashfully.

"DO IT!!!" they exclaimed jumping up and down. I looked at my sisters who were both glowing, and it wasn't the Fenty Beauty they were wearing. The sisterly advice they were giving me actually rang true. I was so focused on what others thought of me, I never paid attention to what I knew to be true.

"I'm going to do it! Tomorrow, I'm going to tell Coach Smith I want to join the team, no matter what *anyone* says!"

"Good, now if only we could get you to dress better!" Amani said, looking me over.

"I have to agree. Allah calls for modesty, not frumpy and... whatever *this* is," Amara said, pinching my parachute pants.

I pushed past my sisters to grab my basketball with a laugh and tossed it in the air. "Y'all up for a game?"

"Let's do it!" they said in unison. Our laughter carried on through the late afternoon and into the night. With the help of my sisters and my friends, I knew I could conquer anything. I had stood up to my lifelong bully and stood up for what I knew was right. There was a lot more fight in me than I could have ever imagined. It was time I embraced it all. It was a long time coming, but this new version of me was here to stay.

Libby Gray

"Is everyone good?" Kenzie asked, smiling on video chat. After a two-hour conversation, everyone's mind was finally clear. Each of the girls had received beautiful revelations in their personal lives and I couldn't have been happier for them.

"Yes, but I am going to need you guys a lot over these next couple of months," Janais said, laying down in her bed. "I will definitely need help getting adjusted to this new idea of normal."

"I understand that," Adeema squealed. "I'm going out for basketball and I have to find a way to tell my dad, but I am finally about to do something I love!"

"Libs, are you good?" Kenzie asked, making a funny face into the camera. "You've been quiet."

"Oh yeah, I'm great. Just tired, that's all. We fought a major villain yesterday, remember?"

"That's true," Adeema said, hugging her basketball. "Well, ladies I have to get ready for school tomorrow. The rest of my life starts once I walk through those Ridgewood doors." It really warmed my heart to see her so happy. She deserved it.

"Goodnight, Royal Elite Squad!" Janais said, waving into the camera.

"Besos, beauties," Kenzie said, blowing a kiss.

"Night," I said, finally hanging up. I tossed my phone on my bed and laid back. I inhaled deeply and held it for as long as I could, before releasing it slowly.

"LuLu," I said, patting my bed. She hopped up and I wrapped my arm around her as tight as she would allow. Instantly, everything I had been holding back came flowing out in the form of tears. I didn't even know why I was crying, but it felt so good.

"Telling LuLu all your secrets again?" CJ asked, tapping at my door.

I quickly wiped my cheeks, trying to erase the evidence of a soul that was in a world of pain. I forced a smile and sat up. "You know me and Lu!" I said trying to laugh. "She is my girl!"

"You know that she's supposed to be a family dog, right?" he joked, giving her a rub. "But I think she likes you best."

"Can you blame her? I'm amazing," I said, rubbing her belly. "What brings you by?"

"I just wanted to make sure you were okay. That was a really bad argument earlier with Mom and Dad."

"Oh, I'm good," I said, hopping up from my bed and fiddling around aimlessly. "No issues here."

"Libs, for real—it's okay if you're not okay. Our family is going through a lot right now. You don't have to hold it all in."

I gave a shrug. "I promise! What Poppa and Ma have going on has nothing to do with me."

'Okay. Just making sure." He came over to kiss my forehead and gave me a tight hug. I didn't want him to let go, but I knew if I asked him to stay longer, he would know something was up. He walked out the room and I was left alone with my thoughts. The silence rang so loud, it was deafening.

"Music!" I said, grabbing my phone and hitting play on Spotify. "Yes, music will help." A 90s pop song bumped through my speakers and I sang loudly to N'Sync for a while, finally beginning to feel like my old self again.

Poppa stumbled into my room, slurring his words in a way that made it seem like he was speaking in cursive. "STORM, what did I tell you... about... this crap!"

I grabbed my phone quickly and turned the music off, scurrying to the other side of the bed. "I'm sorry, Poppa," I said, unable to make eye contact.

"You never listen!" he said, tripping into my room. "What's wrong with you, huh?"

"Nothing," I said, trying to fight tears but failing. "I'm sorry."

CJ barged in the room quickly, standing between us. "Come on, why are you doing this? You don't want her to see you like this!"

"It's *her* fault! She... she don't listen!" Poppa said, pointing at me. It was becoming too much. I wanted to get away. I had the ability to transport myself anywhere I wanted and I couldn't even use it.

"I'm sorry, Poppa. I really am! Please don't be mad at me!" I pleaded. Mom ran into my room, reeking of a crying fit of her own.

I tried to run to her, but was cut short when Poppa grabbed my arm. "Chase! Let her go!" Mom screamed.

"You're hurting me," I cried, trying to break free.

"She's my child too, Jane!" he yelled, squeezing tighter and tighter. I was in a tug of war with my parents and I was the one who was losing.

"GET OFF OF HER!" CJ said, giving him a shove. Poppa threw me down to the ground before swinging on CJ, hitting him square in his right eye. My father never hit us before, so we all stood there stunned for a moment.

"GET OUT! GET OUT MY HOUSE RIGHT NOW!" Mom yelled pushing him towards the door. "I can't believe you, Chase! This is the last straw! I can't do this anymore. GET OUT! I want you out!"

Poppa looked at my mom, who was rushing to my aid. "Finally, you say something that makes sense—best decision you've made these past twenty years! I'm gone! I'm not needed, so I'm out!" He stormed out and the room remained silent until we heard the front door slam shut.

"Baby, I'm so sorry," Mom said, kissing my cheeks and pulling the hair out of my face. CJ was still in a daze. My breaths became faster and faster. My hands were shaking. I looked around the room and tried to center myself, but nothing was working. I jumped up and pushed Mom out the way and started screaming at the top of my lungs.

The perfect room that Poppa had made me keep was nothing but a fancy jail cell and I couldn't take it anymore. I began wreaking havoc—throwing pictures off the wall, pulling clothes out my closet and pushing things over. I just couldn't keep it together any longer. "I can't stay here! I need to leave! I gotta go! I can't breathe!" I screamed, crying uncontrollably.

"Libs, breathe," CJ said, putting his hands on my shoulders.

"I can't... *I can't.*" I had always prided myself on being able to get over things quickly. I was everyone's peace and had the ability to bring joy to everyone's life around me. But right now, at this moment, I couldn't even make myself happy. I grabbed my phone and ran into the bathroom, locking it before anyone else could enter.

"I'm right outside, Libs, and I'm not leaving you," CJ said from the other side of the door. "I'm sitting right here, okay? I love you."

I sat on the floor and placed my headphones in before pushing play. Billie Ellish's "Lovely" featuring Khalid started and sang my heart's tune. I don't know how, but music always had the ability to explain things I couldn't even comprehend myself. As the song played, I was hit with a painful reality: bad things happen, and sometimes, there is nothing that can be done about it. Inside, I was feeling something so painful, I didn't even know it was humanly possible.

I had fought with friends, bad guys and supervillains. I had fallen off jungle gyms, got into accidents, had the stomach flu and so many other terrible things—but I would do all those things again ten times over if would take away the pain of losing Poppa. Laying in my bathroom against the door with a face full of tears, I lacked the ability to see past the moment. I knew I wouldn't be there forever, and even knew my story wouldn't end there on the bathroom floor. But the reality was that this chapter was over, and it wasn't a good one.

I had lost my Poppa for a lot of reasons I couldn't understand. But he was gone. We had gone from a family of five down to four, losing the man that once kept us together. *Growing pains*, I would hear adults say. I assumed this was one of those pains. I just prayed it would make me better. I unlocked the bathroom door as a silent welcome to enter.

My brother and mom flooded inside, both sitting on either side of me.

I laid on my mom and cried as she rubbed my back. "I know, baby, but we will get through this! Like we do everything."

"You're a warrior and a fighter, Libs!" CJ said holding my hand. He started playing "Warrior" by Demi Lovato on his phone, a song I would always ask him to play when I got in his car. I looked at him and smiled. It was the perfect reminder I needed that everything would be okay—maybe not today, but someday soon. And that gave me just enough hope to keep fighting.

About the Author

D.A. Alston is a Georgia resident that was born in San Diego, California. When she's not writing, she's shaping young minds as she has spent the past ten years teaching and tutoring youth from toddlers to middle schoolers.

You can connect with me on:
- http://thedaway.com
- https://twitter.com/da_alston_
- https://www.facebook.com/TheOnly.DA.Alston

Also by D.A. Alston

The Unlikely Tale of the Royal Elite Squad

http://www.vitalnarrative.com/shop/the-unlikely-tale-of-the-royal-elite-squad

116 pp. *The Unlikely Tale of the Royal Elite Squad* is a Young Adult novel that follows four young girls as they embark on an exciting new journey after an accident occurs at their school.